FATED MISTAKE

JAMESON PACK

K.A. BAUER

JUST A HEADS UP:

The events of this book take place simultaneously with the events of the Alpha's Little Psycho series and continue on after the end of the events of those books. If you have not read the series, you should still be able to enjoy this series on its own, but please be aware that there may be some events and scenes that are only explained fully in the other series. There will definitely be crossovers from Ethan and Ric and Jack throughout the Jameson Pack series.

Thank you and I hope you enjoy how Fate works in the Jameson Pack.

1

JOSH

<u>Seven and a Half Years Ago</u>

"Why do I have to be his chosen heir?" I ask Dad for the umpteenth time today. I just don't get why Uncle Edward is so hellbent on choosing an heir right now. He's only in his six hundreds. He's got at least another quarter millennia before he will even consider retirement, so why do I have to leave home to go live with him as his heir?

"My brother needs an heir sooner than expected," Dad repeats with a sigh. "There's a chance that he will want to retire sooner than expected after having lost his grandson. His heart is not in it for being the leader that the Eastern region needs, and your older brothers are too set in their ways to be groomed for the position."

I wanted to ask about my sisters, but I know that is a losing battle. As much as we keep up with technology, vampires really don't keep up with social trends. Misogyny is alive and well with the undead. At least our cousins up in Canada don't make the women be second class citizens until marriage. Mom is still fighting the uphill battle against Dad and Uncle Patrick for that one. At least Uncle Edward allows them their autonomy once they reach maturity.

Are you ready, Joshua?

Think of the devil...

Yes, Uncle Edward. Father has made the arrangements. I will arrive at your manor house tomorrow evening.

I feel the mind link cut off abruptly. He was a whole lot more fun before his grandson died. Ethan was my second cousin, or was it third cousin once removed? I don't really know how the genealogy terminology works. He was Uncle Edward's grandson from the daughter he didn't even know existed until she died. Ethan was left with werewolves to raise because his mother was a hybrid. Because of that fact, odds were that hee was going to have a wolf and needed a pack until he shifted. That happens when a wolf turns thirteen.

It was last month, a few months after my cousin would have shifted, that Uncle Edward found out that Ethan died in a freak accident, along with his adoptive parents. He was supposed to be there for his birthday, but something with the fae delayed him by three months. I think he blames himself and it changed him.

Growing up, my mom and dad made it a point to let me know that I would get to meet Ethan when he came to live with Uncle Edward. I was supposed to be his advisor, his assistant and liaison within the vampire kingdom, which I was totally fine with. I spent my life preparing to be essentially support staff, not the regent. I mean, I am the youngest of all of my siblings and full vampire cousins. As the baby, I should have zero responsibilities.

Now, I'm suddenly being thrust to the top spot and have to learn from the grief stricken shell that used to be my favorite uncle. It's just not fair.

Arms wrap around me from behind and I roll my eyes at the fact that my mother is giving me yet another hug. "My hijo," she sniffles. "I am not ready to give you up to your tío. He cannot have you yet."

"Mama," I sigh and pry her hands away yet again. "Dad and Uncle Edward have already decided. I'm sixteen now and have my abilities. There is no reason for me not to go at this point."

Even if I wanted to escape, I won't be given the option.

It's not like I object to being his heir exactly. I just wanted to stay here at home for a few more years – finish high school with my friends. I might be a vampire, but I managed to convince my parents to allow me to attend the public school instead of the private academy the other supe kids go to. With the rise of television, books, and movies depicting our kinds fully integrating, I think it's only a matter of time before the insular and elitist thinking goes away.

That is probably the biggest reason I'm not fighting this. When I become the king, I can work on integration and make it more seamless, like the shifters and witches have done. They work side by side with humans everywhere, including schools and hospitals.

Of course, it helps that the other supernatural races can be outside twenty-four hours a day without getting a wicked sunburn. A day or two exposure to sunlight won't kill a healthy vampire of any age, but it hurts like a bitch according to my sister Janice. Out of all of my siblings, only I was lucky enough to inherit Mama's bloodline gift of photophilia, which loosely translates as "light loving." Janice and my other siblings only got the psychic stuff from Dad's side of the family.

"Time to go, kiddo," Dad says as he hauls my last suitcase out to the waiting car. "I want to make sure there's enough time for everyone to get back home before sunrise."

I really don't want to say goodbye to the southern California sunshine, but I guess it's time to see what the east coast beaches are like. At least they should be mostly deserted in November, right?

Five Years Ago

Why the fuck did I run away from Uncle Edward?

I have been stuck in this hellhole for at least a year at this point. It's difficult to tell time in here. Shortly after arriving in South Carolina, Uncle Edward pissed me off, trying to force me to stay inside during the day and not letting me finish out high school.

He said human education isn't as important as my training to be a regent.

I said, *"Fuck you!"* and stormed out of his office at the warehouse.

I mean, it was bad enough taking away the sun like I was some *ordinary* sixteen year old vamp, but he also wanted to cut me off from the world that I love. I don't like the messiness of having to take blood to feed, but I hate missing the latest movies and people watching just as much. I was already hurt that I had to give up my passes for San Diego Comic Con, but then he had to forbid me from going out anywhere without guards.

It was too much for me.

So, in a fit of teenage rebellion, I ran to the shopping district for some retail therapy. Instead of finding something worth buying, I found a young werewolf with pain practically screaming from inside of him. I was still getting used to the whole psychic mind link stuff from Dad's side of the family, so I had a hard time shutting the kid out. His anger and story drove me to volunteer to help him find his bestie.

I figured I would be gone maybe a month or two, just enough time to get the point across to my tightwad uncle that I am not a child needing to be coddled.

Unfortunately for me, my dumbass went and got caught by these bigoted extremist humans with a full blown mad scientist fetish. *Way to prove your family right, Josh...*

I don't even remember how these dimwits caught me. I remember going to sleep at the hotel in Columbus, Ohio and when I woke up, I was in this dank and disgusting room. I tried using vamp strength and speed to escape, but somehow, they have the place reinforced. I tried using the mind link to call out to my family. No one answered— At least no one on the outside of this hellhole.

The first few weeks here were complete and total isolation. I think they wanted to starve me into submission, but didn't realize how bad of an idea that is for a teenage vampire. Without any kind of food or blood, I was surely in danger of dying for realsies had they not noticed. In reality, the idiots here almost killed me after they went to so much trouble to get me.

I mean, vamps get their powers at sixteen, but we don't lock into our immortality until sometime between eighteen and twenty-five. It depends on our bloodlines. I come from the two most powerful bloodlines on this side of the world, but it still doesn't change the fact that I'm still too young to be immortal. I think I'm seventeen, maybe eighteen at this point, so I can still die like a human.

It seems I am the only vampire they managed to snag and I've had to suffer through their trial and error comparing what they've read in young adult homo-erotic fan fiction and what actually exists.

That's the other thing about this place. They got a fucking menagerie up in here. Most of wolves in here are betas who are so weak, they don't do well without an alpha wolf around to tell them what to do. The few betas I knew from back home *do* have a backbone wouldn't be dumb enough to get caught. A few other beings here seem to have spirit, but not many of them.

In addition to myself, as the vamp representative, and the wolves, I've encountered a few fae, a siren, and some other species of shifter. I mostly stopped paying attention after about six months. People don't seem to last very long in here and it's better to save my energy for healing rather than remembering.

Despite the constant revolving door of fellow victims, I have managed to make a few friends in here— if you can call being bonded through the trauma of constant vivisections and gladiator style pit fights becoming friends.

Celeste is a halfling fae woman who seems to get the worst of the harassment from the guards, at least in public. All of the guards here are men, and she is the one of the few women who has lasted more than a few weeks. The others either become empty shells or they end up in the mass grave under the basement. I honestly don't know how she handles it every day as a twenty-year-old. Between her and Erica, a she-wolf, I don't know who is stronger for dealing with the monsters.

My other friend in here is Ethan. Ironic, isn't it? He is the same age and has the same first name as my cousin that died. Plus, he is a wolf. When we were first pitted against each other in the fighting ring last month, I wondered if there could be a chance at a miracle, that my cousin was alive after all. But this kid is so freaking tiny and looks nothing like anyone in my family.

Plus, he's an omega wolf. Halfling wolves are never anything but betas, if they even manage to shift, according to the history books. His mother, my uncle's daughter, was a wolf less halfling, so my cousin being an omega, especially one as powerful as Ethan, is something I dismissed pretty quickly after meeting my friend.

A familiar melody pops into my head, but it isn't my voice singing it. What the fuck? Who is singing in my head?

I haven't tried to mind speak with anyone since maybe my first month in here. I got tired of the sobbing and pain I heard in response at the beginning and cut myself off to anyone not blood related. Considering only the Sullivan bloodline, the royal bloodline, is able to use it outside of direct familial connections, I am pretty sure I am losing my mind.

Hello? I send out into the air. Has my family found me? If so, why are they singing songs from a children's movie?

I hear a squeal in my head before I get a response.

The voices are talking back again. Have I finally gone crazy? Well... really crazy, not the kind of crazy I have always been. Like I'm not CRAY CRAY, am I? Is that how you use it?

I can recognize the voice in my head now. Well, not so much the voice as the rambling. This is Ethan, my omega wolf friend who will talk non-stop unless you can redirect his attention to something else and...

FUCK! This means my friend Ethan really is my fucking cousin that everyone thinks is dead.

I have to get out of here and get help. Uncle Edward needs to tear this place apart. Fuck Uncle Edward, we need the whole fucking Sullivan clan.

But wait, if he's here, that means...

Shit.

They faked his death to stop people from looking. Did they fake mine as well?

Hey, Ethan. I send to him. *Shut up. I'm not your crazy talking. This is Sully, your vamp bestie in this house of horrors. Now that we can talk like this, we are going to figure out a way to get us both out of here.*

My mind is going through all of the possibilities of how to escape when the door to my cell opens. Looks like Noah is my escort for today's fun. Steeling myself for whatever is about to happen, I follow the asshole to the room where they like to torture me, to test my limits. I can only hope to keep surviving long enough to get Ethan free of this place.

One Year Ago

"Extensive injuries..." a voice is talking somewhere around me. It doesn't sound like any of the dickwads I've been listening to for the last however many years, but that doesn't mean anything. Occasionally the asswipe in charge would bring in a new doc.

"He's lucky... wake up in time... healing rapidly..."

There is a strange beeping noise in the background. That is new.

Did the fuckwads move me to another facility?!

NO! They can't have done that! I need to be with Ethan! I need to save him!

The last thing I can remember, they were taking me down to the sub-basement after they gutted me. I refused to cooperate when they tried to get me to give a sperm sample. I was willing to do a lot of things in that place to stay alive, *had* done a lot of things I can never take back that will haunt me forever.

But there was no fucking way I was going to accommodate their request to impregnate my cousin. I was raised to respect the choices of those who are blessed with the ability to give birth. I could never take part in something that removed that choice from anyone, let alone a member of my own family.

"Hijo, please," my mother's voice sobs somewhere nearby. "Please don't leave me, mi niño."

My mother is here?

That means...

I made it out of there. I actually escaped.

Opening my eyes is a struggle, but I manage it through sheer force of will. The world is bright, *too bright* after years in darkness. I shouldn't have let them see that the sun didn't burn me. They took it away from me, like they took everything else.

The sight of my family surrounding me is a balm I didn't know my soul needed. Mama is grasping my hand as if she could hold me to this life by sheer force of will. Dad and Janice are by the door, with a man in a lab coat that I assume is a doctor. Uncle Reynaldo is passed out along with my other siblings Joseph, Andrea, and Carlos on those horrid travel cots on the other side of the room.

While I try to wrap my head around the fact that I am free and not just trapped in a vivid dream, I sense movement to my right. Purely by reflex, my body tenses and I try to get into a defensive position. But my wounds are too severe and the pain starts to pull me back under. Before the darkness takes me again, my brain catches up and I realize the movement was only Uncle Edward approaching my hospital bed.

He needs to know about Ethan. He needs to go save his grandson. If those assholes have their way, the damage they manage to inflict on him will be irreversible. It's bad enough that they've been selling his heats to humans, if they get a supe to do it... Someone must save him.

*He's alive...*I send out before my world returns to the blessed void of unconsciousness.

2

MAX

Getting a scabbard for Slash, Little Dude's new sword, is my number one priority today.

The kid gave us all a fucking scare with his whole dying and coming back thing he pulled. Even though he told us about not being able to stay dead when he explained his deal with the goddess, it was hard to see him essentially as a corpse in the bed for the entire month after Jessica killed him. Not gonna lie, I hate that bitch for not saving him for real. His inability to die is just another form of torture.

I thought Ric was going to waste away next to Ethan's corpse. To be honest, I wasn't too far behind him. Then, with no warning, Ethan is suddenly back in the land of the living and everything is back on track. At least, it's on track for them.

Yep. Back to Ethan being head over heels in love with the Alpha and not me. He always made the goo goo eyes for Ric, but I figured he would eventually look to me like that once he realized how much I love him.

Shake it off, Max!

I need to get a grip. The fates have apparently put Ric and Ethan

9

together, and gods know those two have proven their devotion to each other over the last few months. I thought it was over for them after Ethan's heat, but apparently that was all a misunderstanding. The guilt was killing all of us, so ultimately I'm glad it was cleared up, but now the two of them are stronger than ever.

A text message comes through as I pull up to the custom leather shop where I plan on ordering the scabbard.

> **LD:**
> Can you tell Daddy that ice cream is a requirement for Thanksgiving?

I have to chuckle at the question. Do I spoil the guy? Absolutely. I'm a Daddy... well, I'm a caregiver Dom at the very least. The title itself isn't the important part. But Ethan is an adorable little and deserves to be spoiled rotten after all of the shit that he's gone through.

> **Me:**
> I will talk to him, but you need to listen to your Daddy or you'll end up getting punished

> **LD:**
> Spankings are fun tho

> **Me:**
> I didn't say funishment 😏

> **LD:**
> 💩

I pocket my phone and grab the bundle of cloth that I used to wrap up Slash. I know this isn't going to be the most expensive present he receives for Christmas this year, but I want it to be special. I want to know that he will have a reason to think of me when I finally manage to get up the courage to leave the pack.

I just need to make sure he's safe. He saved me so many times without ever knowing it, and I failed him spectacularly eight years ago. I cannot fail again. Ethan is the only one who has and will ever hold my heart. Even though he loves another, my heart is and always will belong only to him.

3

JOSH

It's gone...

The lab is gone.

There is nothing left except a burnt-out husk of a warehouse outside of Dayton. Years of torture. Years of suffering – and nothing but the shallow grave in the sub-basement remains.

Give those who were buried beneath the building a proper send-off.

I tell the men that Uncle Edward sent with me through the mind link. If I open my mouth right now, I will probably start screaming and won't be able to stop.

But take pictures of their faces and any markings that could be used to identify them. We will need to find and notify families of the victims.

Turning away from the charred remains of my living nightmare, I let the tears fall silently. I was too late. By the time I woke up again, it was months later. I couldn't be certain that anyone else was still alive, so I had to find out first. I couldn't get their hopes up, not without proof that he still lives.

I didn't tell Uncle Edward or my family about Ethan specifically, but I did tell them that there were others still being tortured in the lab. It took almost a year, but I finally managed to convince them that I needed to go back to rescue those who were still there. I rushed back to the hospital where I was found in the morgue and figured out through magic and tracking where the lab was likely located.

Looking at the scene in front of me, it seems I am too late. It appears they scrapped the project or changed locations at least six months ago. Either way, there's nothing left here. They covered their tracks by torching the place.

The only thing I'm worried about now is whether or not Ethan is among the dead. If he is, then I have to come clean. I have to tell my family that I was in there with him and that I failed to save him. If he is not among the dead, my search will continue. I'll track down the assholes in charge and force them to give him up to me. I cannot fail him again.

"Here are the photos of all of the bodies that were intact enough to get identifiers," Chase says, handing me his phone. "The rest are only skeletons that honestly we are going to need a witch to tell what bones belong to which body at this point."

I wipe at my face before facing the vampire. He has been assigned to me as a personal bodyguard. Chase is only fifty years older than I am, but in vampire terms, he's practically my age. He has listened to almost every gory detail about this place when I can't hold back and have to share. He has been the one who has held me, well more like restrained me, when the nightmares come. I have almost killed him in my terror three times already, but for some reason he keeps showing up.

The only thing he doesn't know is the fact that my *friend* that I left behind is actually my cousin. My cousin who also happens to be the prince he was raised to be protecting initially. I'm the default, the backup prince. It was never supposed to be me.

Everyone on this mission knows that I am searching for the ones that were left behind when I escaped. No one knows that their true prince is the one I am hoping to find.

"Get the doc to do dental impressions on the skulls and take DNA samples off each of them," I tell him as I turn back to the building. "After we have that, let the witches do their thing if we can't find a match through science. We *will* find out who they were and make sure no family is left without answers. But I don't want the witches to spread word about the number of bodies here. We don't need to have rumors out there about our family's inability or unwillingness to protect the other races."

Uncle Edward is going to have enough to worry about when I find Ethan...

As Chase heads back to relay my orders to the rest of the team, I start flipping through the photos. It is a punch to the gut every time I recognize a face. I knew so many of them. Granted, I didn't get close to them like I did with Celeste and Ethan, but there was still a connection formed between all of us in there. Torture really bonds people, ya know?

I pause when I reach a photo that makes me smile. Flipping to the next one, I feel the corners of my mouth raise even higher. I feel a bit evil for finding joy in the sight of a dead body, but the feeling is there nonetheless. The fact that the men who gutted me and tried to throw me into that pit ended up there themselves is the very best kind of karma. I just wish I knew who put them there so that I can shake their hand.

"You okay, Josh?" Chase asks as he approaches. "That right there is a Jack Torrence smile and it's kind of worrying me."

He surprises a laugh out of me with the movie reference, and it breaks me from the dark and twisty feelings that were building inside of me. We did a Stephen King movie marathon for Halloween last week and he got totally freaked out by the old Kubrick movie with Jack Nicholson. I couldn't believe he had never seen it.

"Redrum," I grate out as I do the little finger curl thing the kid does in the movie. All of the guys chuckle as Chase visibly shivers in response. For a big bad vampire, he gets really squeamish with human horror movies.

"The two that I highlighted," I tell him, handing back the phone, relieved to find that neither Ethan nor Celeste is among the dead, "They don't get proper rights. They were among the staff that treated us as less than animals. Give their bodies to the demons for a good price."

Chase flips through the photos and sends them to the rest of the crew with my instructions. The demons will make good use of their parts for spells and charms and potions that the warlocks and witches might need. The body parts of murderers and rapists can be extremely powerful tools for magic as long as the negative energies are properly processed. The demons know how to do that safely.

"Are we making a deal with the demons or just selling?" Chase asks as we head toward the car.

The idea makes me pause for a second. I could use a deal to try and get a lead on where they might have moved the lab, but there's no guarantee that a lower-level demon wouldn't get captured the same way I had been years ago. Hell, from what I could tell, they might have even been able to hole a mid-level one. I would never subject anyone to that...

"Just sell," I say as I climb in the back of the SUV. "I don't want to trap us in a deal over something like this hellhole. Plus, I want to make sure I have a personal hand in their takedown when the time comes."

My bodyguard nods and closes the door to the backseat. When he gets in the driver's seat and heads back for the highway, I finally let myself feel what I've been holding back.

I will find you, cousin. I never meant to abandon you to save my own life.

I promise I will find you again and make it right.

4

JOSH

<u>February</u>

The proximity alarms are going off for the warehouse again. I swear those dumbass beta jock meatheads from the Heartstone Pack will never learn. The idiots don't seem to understand that we are fucking vampires. There is only so much disrespect and trespassing that we will put up with before the excuse of young and dumb stops applying. Pulling up the camera for the parking lot, I see the same three shit-stains as usual pulling an unconscious boy from the back of their truck.

If the kid is older than fifteen, I'll swallow piss. This time they have gone too far. I don't even switch over to the closer feed before I make the decision. I'll find out what our king wants us to do to handle it, but there is no chance I'm not acting on it this time. Unfortunately, human laws and morality don't always apply with Uncle Edward, so I need to gage his level of interest in their punishments.

Uncle? I send over the mind link. I hate to interrupt his dinner, especially considering he is finally getting back to regular feedings after years of neglecting his health, but taking care of these betas is going to cause an issue with one of his few friends. He doesn't make them easily, so if I can salvage the relationship between him and Bennet Heartstone, I will.

What is it, Joshua? I was just about to partake in a delightful oger halfling for a snack. Might you wish to join me for a change?

I cringe at the thought. I haven't been able to smell blood, let alone ingest it, at all since getting out of the facility. Thankfully, I have my mother's ability to process the energy from the sun; otherwise, I would be weak as fuck surviving on only human food. Vampires need the magic of life from blood or another source to power our bodies as supernaturals. Without it, we are basically just immortal humans.

No thanks, I send back to him. *But the fuckwad betas from Heartstone's pack are back at the warehouse...*

Language, Joshua! Of course, he interrupts me just to lecture me on my word choice. *A regent needs to be mindful of his audience and avoid profanity, even within his thoughts.*

I grimace. What the fuck difference does it make what words I use. They *are* fuckwads. I don't have the time to go get a dictionary to find a suitable replacement word to satisfy his Victorian sensibilities. Unbidden, a smirk forms while I listen to his scolding. I can't wait until I find Ethan and he gets to hear the mouth on his grandson.

Whatever, I interrupt before he can really get on a roll. *The betas brought an unconscious boy with them and they're currently playing rock, paper, scissors for the opportunity to do something to him. Unless you want to have to cover up the fact that a literal child was kidnapped, assaulted, and/or raped on our property, I think we need to take care of this pronto and my word choice is a secondary fucking issue!*

I can feel his anger at my defiance, but I don't give a fuck. I glance back at the monitor and see the last of the betas enter the office where they put the kid. They are all inside with him now, but I can't bring myself to log into the feed for the office. I can't watch what they are doing to him, not if I intend to be of any help.

"Chase!" I call for my guard and friend. He rushes into my office, ready to attack. At seeing me perfectly fine at the desk, he cocks his head questioningly.

"I need you to get to the warehouse ASAP. My uncle's office," I tell him as I start shutting down the equipment in the office. "Help the boy in any way that you can. I'll be there as soon as the computers are shut down."

He uses his vamp speed to disappear from the office. I know he will make it to the warehouse in under a minute. If only computers were as fast as us. I can't risk any of the information in this office being easily accessible if someone should happen to come in here.

Joshua, my uncle's voice cuts in before I grab my coat to follow Chase. *I will handle things at the warehouse. You do not need to come down.*

What the fuck? First, the guy doesn't want me interrupting his dinner and now he doesn't want to let me go make sure that kid is alright. I need to see for myself how badly I failed him. It's just another sin on my worthless soul.

I pull up the security feed for the office on my phone. Having the extra security makes sense when you consider it is the office of the King, but waiting for the app to bypass all of the encryptions makes me anxious. What the fuck am I going to see in there?

When the app loads the live feed of the office, I pick my damn jaw up off the ground. If breathing was still a necessity for me, I would be passing out right about now. The room on the screen is coated in blood and gore. The corner of the camera lens is obscured by something sticking to it. Lucky for my sanity, the room is still dark enough that it is only showing in grayscale under the night vision. Full color would have easily triggered a panic attack with the sheer volume of blood that has been spilled.

There is no choice, not really. I'm the future regent, right?

I have to go down there and find out what happened. If that kid is dead because of my inaction, I need to know. Not like I need another reminder of how much of a failure I am, but one thing I know is that I *need* to face this. If I can't face the blood in that room, the blood on my hands, I can't be the heir for the vampires of my uncle's kingdom.

5

MAX

Tearing down the highway with Connor and Ric in the backseat of Ric's Navigator, I have to fight to keep my wolf contained. If it wasn't for the fact that my Alpha commanded me to be the driver for this, I would be tearing Seb a new asshole right about now. He was supposed to be watching Ethan. There should have been zero opportunities to lose sight of the Alpha Mate, especially since Little Dude has been warned multiple times not to use his super speed anywhere humans can see.

Now, thanks to my warrior's extreme fuck up, Ethan not only disappeared from school, but he somehow ended up at the vampire king's headquarters. This is the second time Ethan has slipped away from Seb and ended up in a bad situation. There will *not* be a third.

My Alpha absolutely hates vampires and has never been quiet about it. For his mate to be on their turf, they could use it as an excuse to wipe us all out. Dealing with vamps is like dealing with the mafia. They have a hand in everything, but if you keep out of their way, you'll generally be alright. I personally don't care for them one way or another, but if they do anything to hurt Ethan, I will destroy them all.

Pulling up at the warehouse, Ric orders me to stay with the car while he goes to find Ethan. I sometimes wonder if he knows I am in love with his mate with how often I'm ordered to stay behind or bear witness to them being lovey dovey. It's just another reason I seriously consider leaving this pack behind every so often. It hurts to have my heart broken daily, but it's not enough to leave him behind.

I watch from the car while my Alpha and his Beta talk with the head vampire, King Edward Sullivan. The animosity that Ric is showing to the vampire should get us all killed, but for some reason, the vamp in question decided not to take offense.

I guess it's our lucky day because the king seems to be in a good mood. Connor seems to be doing most of the talking, which is a *very* good thing in this instance. At least the Beta of the Jameson Pack has a level head. None of the rest of us do.

The door to the warehouse slams open causing me to open the car door to jump out and protect my packmates. I only manage to stop myself from rushing forward by sheer force of will. Something is driving my wolf to rush over, but I hold him back. Usually, he is adamantly reminding me that Ethan is Ric's mate, not ours, but something today seems to be pushing his protective instincts to the front. My heart, my head, and my wolf all seem to have different ideas when it comes to Ethan.

Mine, growls my wolf and the cracks widen in my heart.

Even with my heart fully committed, my head knows that Ethan is not ours. Typically, my wolf is on the same side as my head, but he seems to have switched sides today.

Mate!

I hang my head and take a deep breath.

Ethan is our Alpha's mate, not ours!

I tell my wolf for the same thing I have to tell myself every damn day.

The bang on the hood of the Navigator has my head popping back up. In my inner struggle, I failed to notice Ethan showing up. The bang was caused by him rolling around on the hood with an unknown vampire. I jump out of the car door, about to rip the damn undead shit apart when his scent hits me – fresh buttery popcorn with a hint of chocolate and peanut butter.

My mind flashes back to sneaking into the single screen movie theater as a kid. The teenager who worked at the concession counter would sometimes sneak me in and give me snacks at the end of the night, locking me in so that I had a safe place to sleep for a change. She saved me in more ways than one.

MATE! My wolf shouts smugly at me.

The extra seconds of confusion caused by scenting my mate is enough for me to grasp the truth of the situation. This new vampire is my mate, but he also seems to know Ethan. Both of them are smiling radiantly as they come apart. It is like the sun just broke through after weeks of rain.

"How are you alive?" Ethan asks him as they slide off the hood of the car, leaving behind a dent that will make Ric's left eye twitch when he gets the repair bill.

Little Dude looks happier than I have ever seen him outside of Christmas morning, just a couple months ago.

"It wasn't easy and I was hurt pretty badly," the vampire tells him before switching over to Ethan's mind speak thing. I guess it makes sense the vamp would know Ethan can do that if they know each other. My gaze flits between my mate and Ethan, trying to gauge the conversation. Judging by the grins and smiles, it's nothing too bad.

"How are YOU alive?" the vampire asks Ethan before glancing back at Ric, Connor and his king. "You get your rescue from your big brother? Get your kisses from his best friend?"

Ethan pushes him away playfully, and I can't help but feel the sting of jealousy at the knowledge that the man I loved for so long never even thought of me as a possible savior, let alone someone he would want to kiss. There is a flash of something like pain that moves across the vampire's face before he gets admonished by his king out loud.

"Of course, Uncle Edward," Joshua, says with a bow. I'm grateful the king spoke up or else I would never know the name of my mate. My wolf keeps chanting his name like a reverent prayer... *Joshua. Joshua. Joshua...*

"Sorry, Gramps. Etiquette and me just don't mix so I don't mind Sully being a bit of a dick," Ethan calls back to the ancient vampire and pretty much everyone in the vicinity lets out an audible gasp at his audacity.

Leave it to Little Dude to incite a fucking war...

6

JOSH

While everyone else is appalled and clutching their pearls at Ethan's outburst, I'm struggling to hold back my laughter. I still can't contain the joy I feel that my cousin is not only alive, but that he is here and with his mate. From the time we figured out we could talk to each other in the mind speak, we shared our dreams of the perfect outcome. His was always that his big brother would rescue him, and that the Alpha Heir, Alaric Jameson, would be his first real kiss.

My perfect outcome was that I would escape and lead an army back to the lab to save him. I failed in that one, but the one I told him while we were in there was that I would be blessed by fate with a mate who would put me before everyone and every duty.

Since *my* dreams have obviously failed, I'm ecstatic that Ethan's have come true. He deserves everything he's gotten since getting out of there. At least that's what I think until I see the fear blooming on his face.

Ethan drops to the ground and starts tearing his own hair out, making the kind of noises I haven't heard since I escaped. I try to console him, but he only screams louder. Even in the lab, I never heard a sound like that, not from him. Never from him. He laughed. He swore. Hell, he created new profanity as far as I could tell. But this is...

This is *wrong!*

I back away in abject terror. I don't know what to do! *What the fuck did they do to him after I wasn't there?* He was the one who didn't break! They broke *me* because I'm weak. Ethan is the strongest person I know. If he is like this, what hope is there for me to recover?

I can do nothing but watch as his brother and mate get him into the car with the assistance of the warrior they brought as a driver. Once Ethan is out of sight, I finally notice my blood is calling out to someone in the area. My heart yearns to find who it is, but I force myself not to think too deeply on it.

I don't need a mate. I'm not yet twenty-four and kinda don't want to burden some innocent bystander with the fucked up situation going on up in my noggin.

I look to my uncle to see the anguish in his eyes, and it reinforces my decision to not pursue my mate right now. Or maybe I should? I don't want to live with the regret of losing them, right? I am so confused, but Ethan's screams still echo in my mind, drowning out all other thoughts.

Alpha Jameson and Connor Sinclair come back over to where we are, leaving Ethan in the vehicle with their warrior— the one who I am pretty sure fate has set to be my mate. It takes an effort to pull my eyes away from the car, but I somehow manage.

I'm only worried about my cousin, of course.

"Thank you, King Edward," Connor says. "For taking care of my brother and not finding fault..."

Uncle Edward waves his words away. The way my uncle keeps everyone else so ignorant makes everything so much more difficult than it needs to be. The wolves apparently don't even know that Ethan is a member of our family. My eyes drift back to the car and the shame of it all engulfs me.

If only I hadn't run. If only I was there to protect him. If only I had gotten back to him faster...

Alpha Jameson shoots me a dark look before going off to the side with my uncle. Without the distractions, my brain finally registers the scent of the blood from the warehouse. I can't stay here any longer or everyone will know my secret. With one last look at the car, I take off.

Heading for the coast, I need the water to wash it all away. I need the open air and the uninterrupted night sky. In my mind, I am back in that tiny room, suffocating in the darkness. The pain of it all gets to be too much, and I know it will pull me under soon.

I need you, I send out using my mind speak ability, intending the message for Chase. He is the only person outside of my fellow captives who knows what I went through and how it's warped me. He is the only one who I can trust to keep the rest of the world safe while I scream my anguish into the night.

The growl I receive in response is most definitely not from my bodyguard and best friend.

Hours Later

Sitting on the sand, about an hour south of Myrtle Beach, I stare out at the vast inky blackness of the ocean, letting the water barely skim the tips of my toes. I never actually go in the water anymore. I think knee deep is about the farthest out I've managed since coming back. Drowning for two weeks straight tends to make a guy a little wary of deeper water. But I still enjoy the pull of the tides against my feet. The sounds of the waves lapping up on the shore is soothing in a way that no white noise machine or recording could ever replicate... and I need it tonight.

For the first hour that I was here, Chase sat with me, holding me tight against his side while I screamed in an attempt to purge all of the anguish and guilt I was feeling for my cousin. The strong young man with a sharp tongue and backbone of steel is gone. In his place is that broken little boy.

And it is solely my fault for leaving him alone in that place. They broke him worse than they broke me. I can at least live a mostly normal life, as long as I don't have to live among the vampires all of the time. He cracked under a single moment of the expectation of a punishment.

The sound of a motorcycle reminds me I need to breathe. Vehicles mean people which means I need to pretend that I want to appear alive. It used to be so easy, but now I struggle to find a reason to keep up the pretense. I usually make an effort around the others, breathing and pushing my heart to beat a little faster. It makes them more comfortable and less likely to see the truth— that I would rather have been with the others in that basement than face the endless future with the memories branded into my psyche.

It will be dawn in less than an hour, and Chase has had to abandon me to save his own literal skin. As much as it sucks that he won't have full immunity from the sun for another hundred years or so, I relish the time I get to myself most days. When I'm alone, I don't have to bother acting alive when I wish I was dead. If only my death would fix things instead of fucking them up worse for my family, I would take my life in a heartbeat.

Speaking of heartbeats, I can feel one approaching me, strong enough that it feels like his heart beats for both of us. Knowing how dead I truly am on the inside, it might just have to.

"So fate thinks we would be a good match?" a delicious voice comes from behind me. Oh boy. I never understood the descriptor of panty dropping when it comes to voices before this moment, but if I wore them, they would not have just dropped, they'd be disintegrated.

I don't bother turning around to look at him. I know he is the warrior who was taking care of Ethan earlier. My brain supplies the images directly to my brain while I stand up, brushing the sand from the back of my jeans. I'm not sure how much of what I'm picturing is from memory or years of sneaking my sister's romance novels when I first discovered I was more or less gay.

"So how are we supposed to do this thing?"

I feel my fangs lengthening when I turn and look up at his six foot something ultra tan hunk in front of me. I'm five ten and my forehead barely reaches his chin. I could actually climb him and...

Wait... what the fuck?

The feeling of my fangs coming out is foreign to me after so long of the thought of drinking being revolting. I shake my head to clear my mind. I need to think clearly. I need to make sure that this man knows how fate screwed up, that I'm used goods. I'm not good for anyone. I'm broken in a way that will never be fixed.

He is an alpha wolf. He deserves a mate that can give him heirs, not nightmares. There is no such thing as a vampire omega and surrogacy only works with pure vampires. He can do surrogacy with anyone else if he wants.

I can't even offer him immortality. Turning other species is a rare gift that requires witchcraft along with a specific bloodline, and my father eliminated the last of those ones shortly after I was born because of what they did to my Aunt Rosalind.

I have nothing to offer this man...

My fangs don't seem to want to retract. The thought of losing control frightens me, so I open up my mind to tell him that I need more time. I can't promise him forever when I don't know how to face anything farther than this new day. The real reason I prefer the sunrise over the the sunset is that I need the reminder now that there are new days, not endings.

Opening up the mind link, I prepare to explain, but before I can send anything, I catch his thoughts:

How does fate match me to this vampire when I've always been in love with Ethan? He suffered so much, and I've always been there for him. I can't have a mate that will pull me away from him. I need to be there for him. I mean, who else is going to understand?

All the guilt I feel towards my cousin falls away to be replaced by searing jealousy. Who the fuck is he to steal my mate from me?! Fate gave this man to me, only for him to want Ethan. Yeah, that seems to fall in line with my fucked up life.

"You're right," I say turning away from the man that fate fucked me over by pairing me with him. I wish my cousin and I never ended up in that lab, but since I can't change the past, I can at least not need to compete with someone who had it worse than me.

The man in front of me is probably the most gorgeous being I've ever gazed upon. Despite my irrational thirst, I take a step back toward the water and tell him, "We should find a way to take care of this mistake. We will never be mates, not in the way either of us deserve. You love Ethan? Go on then and keep him safe. Don't..."

Don't ever let him feel this kind of pain or regret.

Shaking my head, I swallow the sobs that threaten to escape and take off down the beach just as the sun crests the horizon. This is usually my favorite part of the day, the reason I chose to come back to the east coast instead of staying back in California with Mama and Dad. It's a new day, a fresh start, but the only thing I can focus on is my heart shattering.

Why am I always the backup plan? Why am I never first choice?

7

MAX

Staring at the spot where my mate was just a second ago, I watch the sun rise over the ocean as a pod of dolphins jump in the distance. It is a beautiful sight, but I get no joy from it. My wolf is clawing to get out, to chase after the man who disappeared after rejecting us. But I can't move from this spot.

He said I was a mistake...

No.

He said *we* were the mistake. He doesn't want to be mated to me. He said something about Ethan. What was it?

He said I love Ethan...

Shit.

I know he and Ethan were able to do the mind speak thing, but can he read minds like Ethan? If so, I'm fucked. Depending on what point he tuned in to my thoughts, he might have misunderstood what I was thinking.

For fuck's sake, even if he heard it correctly, I'm not exactly a ringing endorsement of a prospective happy matehood. I spent the entire three hour drive out here debating how in the hell I could possibly manage to be mates with a vampire while being head warrior for Ric. Then there's the issue of how I could be a good mate to anyone when my heart still feels something toward the Little Dude.

It's not like I even have a chance with Ethan. I know that whole-heartedly. So why would Joshua think Ethan is a possibility for me?

"I wish I could kill you," a deep voice growls out of the darkness behind me. I whip around, claws out in a half shift that even my Alpha doesn't know I can do. Only the most powerful wolves can manage a partial shift like this, and I don't like to advertise my strength. I sometimes get the feeling my wolf isn't happy to be under Ric's command, but I don't need one of my very few friends to think that I'm a threat.

The vampire in front of me could be Thor's body double: tall, blond and jacked with muscles to make even straight dudes drool. As much as I love me a piece of eye candy, I feel nothing but trepidation looking at him. He is giving me a cold stare, and something tells me it ain't because I'm trespassing on private property.

"Not your problem, dude," I retract my claws and turn for where I left my bike. "I'll get out of your hair, get back to where I belong. No need to make a big deal out of it."

He grabs me by the elbow and forces me to face him. I hold back my growl when I see the anger flicker to pain on his face. The skin of his arm that the sunlight is touching is already bright red and starting to blister.

"You have no right to judge him," he forces out through clenched teeth, pulling his arm back into the little bit of shadow he's managed to find. "Since you know his cousin, you might have at least an idea of the shit he went through in that place for half a decade. A quarter of his life was nothing but the torture in that shithole."

My wolf snarls at the thought of our mate being tortured. I know Ethan has shared with me some of the things he had to deal with, mostly not voluntarily. But he's told me more than anyone else. Some of the experiments Ethan faced were terrible, designed to kill, and he only survived because of the damn deal with the bitch of a goddess. That doesn't even cover the fucked up breeding room Little Dude described to me.

Wait a second...

"A quarter of his life?" I ask the Adonis in front of me. "How old is Joshua?"

The vampire gives me a cold look and answers, "First of all," he says. "It's Josh, or Sully, to his friends. Only people who don't really know him call him Joshua, with the exception of King Edward. And with him usually it's reserved for when he's in trouble or in unknown company.

"Second, he's only a few years older than your Ethan. He was a toddler when the true prince was born and as the closest pure vampire in the family age-wise, Josh was raised with the understanding that he would be Ethan's advisor and protector.

"Ethan was supposed to come live with his grandfather, King Edward, when he turned thirteen. I was assigned as the full time security for both Ethan and Josh the week before the king was scheduled to pick up his grandson. I was placed into a year long training regimen to prepare. Josh was to join us once he finished high school out in L.A."

Based on what this vampire is telling me, this means Joshua, Josh, is only in his early twenties. Some vampires don't become immortal until almost thirty. He might not even be fully immortal yet...

That means he was even more vulnerable than Ethan in that place. Holy fuck, I could have lost him before I ever found him.

"Josh became the sole heir when King Edward was told that Ethan had died in a fire. At that time, Josh had his whole life torn away from him. He was pulled from his school ahead of schedule and brought here. From what I understand, he and the king did *not* see eye to eye on the subject of his schooling. The day before I arrived for my position as his guard, he ran away."

School. Pulled out of school?

He was a fucking teenager! And vamps come into their powers at sixteen, so was this before or after he got his abilities?

"We only found him by chance," the vampire in front of me says quietly. "It was years later when a witch at a hospital in Ohio recognized that the body brought into their morgue was a severely injured vampire and not a corpse."

My body freezes in terror at his words: "*severely injured vampire.*" If a vampire is considered to be severely injured, that means they either almost lost their heart or their head. Vampires regularly laugh off amputations as flesh wounds. The only other reason for an injury to be considered severe is if they are not yet immortal.

I guess the horror is plain on my face because the man in front of me gives me a small smile before explaining.

"He had only just barely locked into his immortality," he says. "His family on both sides tend to be locked in by twenty-five, but it seems the additional trauma made his kick in sooner. Had that not been the case, the lack of blood in his body would have meant certain death. His heart was almost cut in two, and his throat was slashed ear to ear. It took almost two months for him to regain consciousness. And the only thing he got out was *He's alive* through the mind link before falling into a coma for another three months.

"We all thought he was happy to not be dead. It wasn't until he woke again and had full use of his vocal chords that he told any of us that he had left behind friends that he needed to rescue. It took another six months after he woke up the second time, until this past fall, for his family to allow him to return to Ohio to search for them. But all we found was the burned remains of the warehouse that held the lab."

I remember Connor telling me about how he slaughtered everyone inside the building and burned it to the ground when he found Ethan. The look on the Beta's face when he told me about that place... Let's just say, I will do whatever necessary to stay off of Connor Sinclair's shit list after getting a glimpse of the darkness he hides behind that mask of the perfect son.

"There was no one left alive," I tell the vampire as I start to move toward the road and the deeper shade. "Connor, our Beta, was the one to find that place and he went kind of nuts killing everyone who wasn't Ethan. He said he torched the place to take care of any evidence. Guaranteed if you found anything, it was something the fire didn't reach."

The vampire nods as if what I'm saying makes sense. "The only things we found were the bodies buried beneath the basement. For the victims we could identify, we sent their remains to their family if we could locate them. We gave the other victims proper rites and laid those to rest who had no one looking for them."

There is a surge of pride in my chest at how my mate handled such a delicate situation, but I'm quick to squash that. He doesn't want to be my mate. He ran from me. My wolf is howling inside, both of our hearts breaking. But this man in front of me doesn't get to see our pain. I have to hide it.

"So," I ask the vampire in front of me, "How do I go about making things right with Josh?"

He is starting to look a little rosy all over now, even though he is not in direct sunlight. I thought the sun thing was supposed to be just an irritation to them, but it seems like this guy has a severe allergy or something. I know I have seen vampires out in the middle of the day with no more issues than your average fair skinned human, so I can't help but wonder what is going on with this guy.

He hands me a card before walking toward a car idling on the road.

"My name is Chase," he tells me. "You can call me once you figure your shit out. That kid... He's grown up believing everything he has is only because Ethan couldn't or wouldn't have it. His position, his life, his freedom have all been determined by his cousin's existence. Ethan has been the only focus of his life for as long as he's been alive, but at some point he deserves to have it be about him, not Ethan. Either choose him for him or walk away. Don't let him think he's a consolation prize."

I fucked up big time.

But at least I have a chance to fix this. All I have to do is ease up on my time spent around Ethan, and then I can use my time to figure out how to woo a vampire. I mean, the only reason I was even thinking about being in love with Ethan at all today was because of the danger. But he is perfectly safe. He'll spend time with Ric, *his* mate, and then I can focus on winning over my own.

8

MAX

<u>March</u>

It has been a special kind of hell over the last month or so. I'm torn between wanting to find my mate and make things right and my need to protect Ethan. Every day that I witnessed his disappointment in not seeing his Daddy show up has just ratcheted up my rage toward my Alpha. This is *not* how someone should treat their mate!

The guilt and miscommunication between the two of them is going to be the death of us all.

Over the last month, Ethan and I have gotten much closer, but my wolf still wants me to call that Chase guy to get in touch with our mate. I called him right after I got to the Heartstone Pack. After finding out Ethan had requested sanctuary there, I raced over to protect him. But I didn't want to risk Josh to not know where I was, so I called. Chase told me that Josh wasn't ready to listen to anyone about mates yet, so I left him alone for the time being. Now, I'm even more confused.

My heart wants Ethan. My wolf wants Josh. My head goes back and forth. The longer I'm around Ethan without my Alpha, the harder it is to remember that he doesn't belong to me. It got to the point where I suggested to Alpha Bennet that perhaps Ethan should go live in the dorms where he could get a sense of normalcy for once in his life. His mate, Lisa loved that idea and set it up. I am just happy to be able to stay away a bit more, attempt to keep my heart from falling too far again.

Even though the asswipe hasn't reached out the entire time we've been here, Ric showed up at Bennet Heartstone's place today for a meeting regarding something about a letter he received from the fae demanding Ethan.

Fuck that shit!

I was there when the deal was struck for him. I know the terms and who is responsible. Those ugly fuckers won't get their hands on him if I have anything to say about it. I allow the memory to come forward while the rest of the room debates the politics.

Approximately Ten Years Ago

I should have never forgotten my workbook. The options now are to grab it and risk being seen by her or go to school without my work done again and get detention. I don't mind detention so much, but I'm bordering on suspension now. I can't afford to be trapped here with her for days on end. I need school to be able to remember why living is important.

Sneaking in is more difficult than usual today. She apparently threw a bottle at someone after I left this morning. I didn't think she would have clients this early considering how late the last one left. I am going to have to be extra careful. Now, where did I leave the workbook?

There it is! I can see it on the end table.

Houston, we have a problem...

I hear a groan before I fully come into the room. Based on the voice, I am pretty sure the Alpha is here and ew, they're just getting started. I can't get my workbook without them seeing me. I'll need to hide and wait for them to go to the room.

At least, I hope they go to her room. I don't want to think about my mother and the Alpha getting it on where I sleep.

I manage to squeeze my body into the pantry only because the damn thing is always empty. There's no point in me stocking it. She'll just leave everything open to rot in her drug induced hazes... or throw it at my head when I refuse to give her my money.

At least the empty shelves work in my favor since my last growth spurt. I need the extra room for my shoulders now. Sixteen hit really hard with the hormones and the height. My shoulders are starting to get wider, but luckily malnourishment keeps a guy trim.

I barely control the sound of my surprise and the thump of my head on a shelf when the front door crashes open. Who the fuck did she piss off now?

She can't find out I'm home or she'll try to use me as a bargaining chip again. I might be bigger now, but I'm still not an adult. Nor have I found a decent replacement for the knife I gave to Ethan yet. It's not that easy to find a good blade when you're underage and they keep them locked up. I lifted that one off one of my mother's clients, but most of her johns these days don't carry blades.

"Hello, Alpha," says a voice that's almost musical. I can't tell if it's a man or a woman, but I feel chills run down my spine at the sound of it. I don't trust whoever this is that is talking. I am absolutely certain I don't want them to know I am here.

I hear a scuffle from the direction of the hallway and I'm too afraid to see what it is. I'm struggling to make myself as small as possible.

"Woman, you should offer refreshments to your guests, don't you know that?" says another voice. This one is more masculine, but less terrifying. My wolf is telling me that this one is at least honorable, whereas the other is the one we do not want finding us.

Oh, shit! There's nothing in the house. If the stupid bitch opens the pantry, they'll see me. I can't let them see me. I know it in my gut. They can't know I'm here.

"I got water or rot gut," my mother manages to slur out from the direction of the living room. She is so fucking high she doesn't even care that there are strangers threatening her Alpha in her home. "Maybe some saltines if the pest hasn't eaten them."

"Are you offering us refreshments or just listing things?" the first voice asks.

"You can have whatever you want from my house. You find it, it's yours," she says with a bit more oomph this time. "Damn faries," I hear her mumble under her breath while I hear footsteps coming towards the kitchen.

It's a good thing the fae don't have our hearing or else she might have started a freaking war with that comment. Wait... she said anything from her house... that can apply to me. Shit.

Please don't find me. Please don't find me.

They're in the kitchen now. I can see them through the crack in the door from when she fell against it a while back. They are beautiful... almost too much. "Ain't nothing in this world that don't got some ugly in it." I remember my grandmother saying that before she passed when I was little. She always looked at my mother with contempt, but she left us this house.

I watch through the crack as they each snag juice boxes from the back of the fridge. Shit, I thought I hid those better. I got them for Ethan for when he comes over and I need to clean him up. It still happens from time to time and I don't want to risk him getting sick from touching her stuff.

The man, I think he's a man anyways, stops and smells the air right in front of where I'm hiding. I hold my breath and do my best not to move a muscle. The fae want children according to the legends. Even though I'm almost seventeen and a man by wolf standards, I am pretty sure the fae go by the age of the land in their judgments, which is eighteen in America right now.

"What is it?" the first voice asks the other one.

"I think I smell a child, but I can't tell over all of... this," he says indicating to the rest of the room.

"I don't think we would want a child from here," the first voice indicates. "Although, I'm tempted to rescue the child to save them from that waste of a woman out there."

I finally let out my breath as they leave the kitchen. The Alpha is crying and begging but I can't really understand what he's saying. I hear a slap and it's silent.

"You brought them into my home, so you will do what is needed for them to get the fuck out!" my mother screams. She slapped her Alpha? She could die for that...

"Fulfill the debt you incurred, Richard son of Alistair," the first voice tells him. "Your son or you. It's your choice."

What the fuck?

"He is my heir!" the Alpha cries out. "I cannot leave the pack without an heir! Plus, he's too old for you to really take in. You need someone young and flexible and already subdued, right?"

"You promised a first-born son of an Alpha!" the second voice booms out. It shakes the house and I think I've just pissed myself.

"And you shall have one," the Alpha says seemingly more confident. "The boy I will give you is the firstborn of an Alpha, but he has no blood family to claim or protect him. He also looks to present toward being an omega."

Who the fuck can he be talking about? We don't have any other Alpha's children in the pack. The closest any of us come to another alpha is Connor and myself. We're alphas, but not of Alpha blood. Connor's family has been the Beta family for generations. As for my father, my mother says he is a warrior in a pack out west and will come for her once I'm grown. If it wasn't for the fact that only a fated or marked mate can knock up a she-wolf, I would wonder about it. But honestly, I'm counting down the days until the bitch leaves me behind.

And as for omegas, our pack hasn't had one of those for multiple generations. I've looked it up and that's why I'm leaving as soon as I can after I turn eighteen to find one. I've known women won't ever check my box since I was little. Mom just drove home the point over the years. I will only ever be with a man, and never again on the receiving end.

"This child you speak of has no family?" the first voice asks, sounding very interested.

"None that will protect him," the Alpha responds quickly.

"Very well," says the first voice. "When he is of age and you know for certain if he is omega or not, he will come with us and your debt will be paid in full."

"Th- Appreciated," says the Alpha. Did this asswipe seriously just promise them a kid to wipe his debt and then almost thank a fae?!

"Oh don't count your blessings just yet," says the second voice. By the *sound of it, I can tell they're heading for the front now. "if you fail to provide the child, you will pay your debt yourself. There are no other chances and no other trades. This child now belongs to us, and none can stop us from claiming him."*

I've tuned out most of the discussion after living the memory again. Drinking seems like a good idea, so I start pounding the whiskey, only responding to let Ric know how I really felt about his father. I still don't understand how in the hell I became friends with Ric considering how much of an ass his father was.

Considering how often Alpha Dick was over the house boning my mom, I was terrified that Ric was my brother. If he had been, that wouldn't be good considering I'm older by a few months. Legitimate or not, the firstborn alpha son is supposed to be the heir. Thank the gods I managed to get a witch to do a DNA test spell on me with him. I don't want to be in charge of anyone, and the elders of this pack are pretentious douchebags who would have forced the issue.

When the DNA came back as *not* a match to Alpha Dick, I swear I didn't come down from that high for days. I am definitely *not* leadership material, at least not when it comes to pack matters. I thought about doing the test using Ric's DNA as a kid but figured the Alpha left enough behind at the house each time that it wasn't difficult to get a sample.

I even tested using Connor's DNA as a kid, hoping I could be one of the Beta's kids. Then, I could be closer to protect Ethan. I was conflicted when that one came back with no matching as well. On one hand, there wasn't a reason I couldn't love Ethan. On the other, I had to respect the rules of the Beta house and family, so I was limited to how much protection I could provide.

Back in the room, Alpha Mate Lisa, came in to force us to take a break for dinner. After dinner, the discussion drags on again, so I zone out while they play the blame game. It's not until a call comes through to the Alpha's phone that Ethan isn't in his dorm room that anything catches my attention. I fucking lose it. It's not smart to blow up at an Alpha in his own home, but this is regarding ETHAN!

He can't get taken again. He's the reason I'm alive. He saved me. I have to save him. I have to protect him. He can't be gone again. I can't live if he's gone. I won't...

I collapse into my Alpha's arms, not caring that he is the mate of the man I love. I barely notice the looks shared between the other men in the room. I don't give a fuck if they know I love him. Ethan needs to be safe. I've already lost what fate blessed me with. *I can't lose him, too...*

9

MAX

The others are talking about something dealing with a witch. They are trying to use magic to find Ethan, but I just want to go blow something up. I need to find him! The only witch I have ever personally spoken to was Ethan's little friend, Shaun, in the year before the fire. Alpha Dick exiled his family right after the big pack move because the kid wouldn't stop saying Ethan was alive...

Look who was right, Dickie boy.

My phone starts ringing and I pull it up to my face, but there's nothing on the screen. I swipe down to ignore the call, but before I can put it back in my pocket, it rings again.

What the fuck kind of glitch is this? The screen is blank again except for the little phone icon to answer.

I decline the call again and set the phone next to me on the couch.

When it rings again, Ric snatches it from my hand and answers the call. The voice on the other end isn't completely unfamiliar, but when he identifies himself as Shaun, I hear the echo of the little nerd that ran around with Ethan. His voice is obviously deeper, but the cadence and tone are the same.

So is the snark.

I feel a sick sort of satisfaction over the next few minutes while

Shaun completely rips apart the Alphas and the vampire king for failing horrendously, when he came to them for help finding Ethan. I would have helped him without question, had I known he was looking, but I didn't come with the pack when they moved initially. I did the dutiful son thing and stayed behind to help my mother get set up in another pack.

Alpha Dick didn't let her move to South Carolina with everyone else. Thanks to her reputation for being entrepreneurial in her sexuality, it took months to find a pack to take her in without me. Okay, that's being nice. My mother was a whore that sold her body to the highest bidder. I was done with the woman but couldn't just abandon her to life as a lone wolf. Call me a softie, but I couldn't just forget about the woman who gave me life and leave her to die.

At least in her new pack she found a chosen mate and stopped being a drunk and a whore. Last I heard, I maybe have a half sibling or step-sibling or something. I cut off all communication after the mating ceremony and wedding. I needed to get back to the Jameson Pack. By the time I returned, Shaun and his family were gone and no one told me anything about why.

"The only person who listened and helped was a sixteen-year-old vampire who didn't want to be the next king," Shaun's voice cuts into my thoughts. "He jumped at the chance to help someone who really needed it... and spent years in that hell himself."

Holy fuck!

He's talking about Josh. My mate was in that hellhole because the men in this room did *nothing* to help this witch search for his best friend. If someone had just listened to Shaun, we could have saved not only Ethan, but Josh as well from that warehouse of horrors.

I think I'm going to be sick.

When Shaun says me and Josh are the only ones allowed to come and guard Ethan, I jump at the opportunity. Even though my heart is struggling with loving Ethan, I need to make things right with my mate. There is a reason fate put us together, and this is an opportunity to at least get to know him better. Ms. Anna always said friends make the best mates and encouraged me to make more friends.

After picking up my *second* favorite little dude, eight-year-old Jack, from the Alpha house, I head to the cabin in the woods. Even though it is awesome that he thought to include his little brother in the protection, I'm still pissed off at Ric. Instead of calling Ethan to apologize and explain himself, he decided to write it down like we're back in middle school. The big bad Alpha is afraid of upsetting his omega mate, so he sends me with a fucking note...

10

JOSH

It's been over a month since I found my mate and realized he is in love with my cousin, who happens to have a mate of his own. Even though I really want to reconnect with Ethan, I am really struggling to get over the fact that everyone in my life has always put his well-being ahead of mine. I understand why, but it still hurts like a bitch.

Before he "died," him being the priority was the only thing I knew. Ethan had his place, and I had mine. I knew who I was in the scheme of things was fine with it.

Then, everything changed. I became the heir to my uncle's kingdom. I went from being trained as an advisor to having to take over completely. I lost my position, my freedom, and my confidence. Because suddenly, I became the what if – the contingency plan no one ever thought would be enacted.

I heard the thoughts of the other vampires and staff in my uncle's house, in our own coven. I heard the thoughts of the packs, clans, and coven leaders when they visited and I sat in on the meetings. They all pitied my uncle for losing his heir and having to choose a replacement to train.

Out loud, they said I was a fine choice, but in their thoughts, they weren't sure I would be able to rise up to the challenge. They were anticipating for me to become a failure of a king. Being the youngest of five, and the third born son, I was merely another spare part as far as the older ones were concerned. The younger ones merely saw in me the fall of the Sullivan Kingdom in the East.

"Hey Josh!" Chase comes running up the beach toward me with my phone raised in his hand. "It's the king."

Not who I want to be dealing with right now. My friend hands the vibrating device to me and says, "I know you said you wanted the hour to yourself, but you know I can't ignore him like you can."

I swipe across the screen to answer the call. I know I've been neglecting my duties over the past month, but he has no room to judge. *His* mate wasn't willing to leave her abusive husband for him and it nearly destroyed him forty years ago. Forgive me if I want to take a few damn months to come to terms with not only being alone forever, but to have to watch my mate pine after my cousin for the next seventy plus years, more if he's a true alpha wolf.

"I need you to go guard Ethan from the fae," Uncle Edward says before I can even issue a greeting. "He is safe enough at the cabin, but you are to go and guard him with Maximillian from Alaric's pack. You will also be there to protect Alaric's younger brother."

I don't even have a chance to say anything before the call disconnects. A text immediately pops up with an address followed by simply, "Go Now."

Great. Not only do I have to go see Ethan and have to act like it's not cutting out my own heart that my mate wants him instead of me, I also have to deal with this Maximillian guy. Knowing Uncle Edward, he's probably some giant meathead enforcer type.

The older generation of my family seems to still think brawn is more important than brains in their guards. One of the first changes I'm making when my uncle retires is finding a way to make being vampire royalty less like running a mafia empire and more like running a modern corporation— same basic principles, but much different window dressing.

"I'm gonna run it, Chase!" I call over to him as I pick up my backpack from the sand. "I'll get there quicker this way and am less likely to bring attention to Ethan's location. I'll reach out via mind link if I need you for anything. Sounds like it's gonna be mostly sitting around for a few days."

Before he can respond, I take off running. Of course, it is going to take almost an hour of running to get there, but at least being tired might help to mask the jealousy. I know it's not likely that I will be able to totally hide it from my cousin. I'll be having a hard enough time dealing with his hurt feelings because I've been avoiding him. I don't want to make him feel guilty for something he has no control over on top of that.

When I get close to the location, I come across a magical barrier and realize why my uncle said Ethan was safe enough where he is. Whatever witch cast this spell is hella strong and knows the fucking loopholes in magic. I step through the warding very slowly, just in case it recognizes me as an enemy. I don't need to get fried by an ally because my vamp speed is seen as aggression.

Unfortunately for me, as soon as I cross the barrier, my blood starts to sing. Fuck my life. Maximillian must be the name of my mate, and of course he is guarding his true love. If I didn't have bad luck, I would have no luck at all.

I open my mind up to scan the area, hoping that there is some *thing* out here that I can go pick a fight with, like a rogue faerie or Bigfoot. Anything is better than heading into the cabin. I pick up some noise and focus on it to see if I can figure out if it is friend or foe.

Ric doesn't fucking deserve him. I've spent these months by his side, yet where was his mate? Sitting on his ass letting Ethan think we don't want him anymore. Fuck that!

No...

I can't do this again. I can't listen to this again. Ethan was happy with his Alpha. What the fuck happened?

My mate's rage is echoing in my head. His entire being right now is consumed by thoughts of Alaric mistreating Ethan. I know what must be coming next. Please, if there is any deity out there who might still favor me, even in the slightest...

Don't let him say it.

There's no future for me if he says it.

If Ric doesn't want him, I'll gladly give him the life he deserves...

My heart stops as I break the connection, throwing up a wall inside my mind. I can't take a breath. My legs give out when I try to run away and I fall to the forest floor just outside of the barrier.

I can't do this. My mate's decision to take another is playing on a loop in my head.

CHASE! I blast out to my friend in desperation. *I need you!*

He arrives in under two minutes and seems to understand with a single glance. I see the horror and pity in his eyes, but it doesn't matter. Nothing matters anymore.

It takes less than a minute for my friend to carry me away from my mate, my family, and my duty. I don't care where we are going, as long as it is away from here.

11

MAX

May

Watching Ethan's smile fall when he saw me instead of Ric when he came out of that motel room is probably in the top three of the worst feelings I've ever had. It ranks right behind being told he was dead the day after he turned thirteen. The top spot that manages to overtake both of those turned out to be getting the letter from Josh that I opened this morning.

Maximillian,

Fate appears to have made a mistake with us. I know you do not love me and it is just a scent/pheromone thing for you. I won't bother you with anything as pedestrian as feelings regarding this unfortunate pairing. I will continue to be civil, for my cousin's sake.

Please do not contact Chase anymore. We will be merely strangers co-existing. For the time being, though, please refrain from coming around Ethan if it is known that I am there, unless it is a group setting. I hope you can keep things civil and refrain from further broadcasting of your feelings for him where I can overhear.

Sincerely,
Joshua Javier Sullivan

I thought Josh was staying away from all of us to give Ethan a chance to recover from everything. According to this letter, he must have heard things from my head that let him know about the struggles within my heart. I had wondered why he never showed at the cabin. Now, I know and feel like absolute shit for it.

How in the fuck do I fix this?

I have a little over twenty-four hours until I am going to be facing my mate for the first time since the night we met. It's not for lack of trying on my part. I have spent the last two months trying to track him down. But after Atlanta, I heard from King Edward that Josh was doing some sort of tour of the territory. Considering their kingdom is the entire eastern half of the country, from the Mississippi to the Atlantic, I was warned it could take a while.

After reading his letter, I am fairly certain he took off to avoid me. But tomorrow will give me a chance to figure it all out. I only need to see him. I need to explain everything to him in person.

I'm floored by a blast of fear from upstairs. It is coming from Ethan, but by the time I get to the door of Ethan's playroom, Ric already has his little boy in his arms. The sight still gives me mixed feelings. I'm glad that Ethan has his Daddy and Ric got his head out of his ass. But at the same time, *I want that.*

Ethan's voice cuts through my mind and I can't help the pain and anger that his thoughts bring to the surface.

He's given up! I send to my wolf who is whining in response to my rage. I can't stick around and watch any more of this. I can't lose him, but I don't know how to fight something like this.

I race outside to my Harley and end up spraying the house with gravel in my haste to get the fuck away before I do something stupid.

How does that perfect little boy get matched with such a self-centered prick?

Why the fuck can't fate put two people together who make sense?

I understand Ethan. We get each other in a way the others just will never understand. We've been through the same kind of shit, so why can't I be the one to help him heal? Why does it have to be that oblivious imbecile?

I start to slow down after I leave the territory since there is no one following me. I have no real destination, but I don't want my men to see my tears. I have completely lost the boy I loved for over a decade to a good man— a dumbass, yes. But Ric is honestly a good man. It's just difficult to get the alpha in me to accept defeat.

A text comes through on my phone. Pulling it out, I see that it's from Ric.

Ric:
My office. One hour

Me:
I've got shit to work out. Is this really necessary?

Ric:
One hour. That's an order.

I send him a thumbs up emoji and put the phone back in my pocket. Turning the bike around, I start back toward the house. I need to come clean with my Alpha and let him decide on my punishment.

12

MAX

"What the fuck is your problem lately?" Ric asks as I enter his office

My wolf growls at the tone we're receiving from our Alpha. It has been taking more effort than usual to get my beast to settle back into a subservient role to his weaker wolf lately. The last few months of denying him of his mate has created an untenable situation that I'm going to need to rectify soon or else I'm going to need to find a new pack.

"Talk to me, Max. You're at the end of the rope here," Ric says in a softer tone. "Your men see that something is up. I can see it. And today, you upset Ethan with your theatrics. If you're not up for the job anymore, tell me. If you want to leave, tell me. Just don't be starting drama and shit in my pack for no reason."

My head drops to my hands, and it just starts to come out.

"I can't keep doing it, Bossman. It hurts to see him so scared and knowing he won't say anything.

"I'm sorry, Ric," I whisper as I lift my eyes to meet my Alpha's. "I didn't know he was your mate when I started to love him."

Ric shoots to his feet with a growl, but I can feel he's holding his wolf back. I continue to tell him how I've been stupidly looking for a way to break a fated bond. I wanted to find a way to set Josh free since he seemed like he didn't want to be saddled with me that night on the beach. I didn't realize he heard my thoughts and misunderstood everything. Well, not everything but enough that he feels unwanted. He doesn't deserve a shit show like me.

"My mind was on Little Dude," I tell Ric regarding how things got so fucked up with Josh. "In my defense, I've always had my mind as my safe place to say what I couldn't say out loud. I could love or hate whoever I wanted there. Even though I had already resigned myself to the fact that I will never be with him... my mate managed to see it all..."

Or at least enough to get the completely wrong idea about how I felt about fate giving him to me.

Ric looks horrified. As an Alpha, I'm sure he's worried about the political side of things. So, I tell him, "He hasn't told anyone that his blood sang for me. No one knows we felt the sparks when he brushed against me leaving me on that beach. And since vampires don't have omegas, there won't be a pregnancy, even if we do somehow end up having sex. We just need to break the bond, and no one will ever need to know."

Ric starts yelling at me loud enough to wake the dead. Thank goodness the office is soundproofed...

"Fate has given you to each other and you're throwing it away because he saw in your mind that you loved his cousin before you even knew he existed?!"

"Love... present tense," I say with steel in my voice, my wolf adding challenge to my tone. "I'm tired of hiding it. I have loved him since the first time I saw him. I've wanted to... no NEEDED to be his shield, his protector, his safety. Jackie being born is the only reason I didn't end my life when we lost Ethan nine years ago. I couldn't let another innocent suffer at the hands of your father...

"After Dick died, I was going to leave since the threat was gone, but by then the little shit had a grip on my heart. I resolved to stay until Jack gets his wolf. At least with a wolf, he can protect himself for the most part."

I explain how my feelings came back slowly over time since Ethan came back and that I had mostly accepted my place in his life until

52

Christmas happened. I was blown away by the thought and care he showed with his presents.

"The holidays made me fall deeper for him. I mean, no one else ever understood the real me and was willing to break the law just to get me gifts I would truly appreciate."

Neither of us hold back from smiling at that. Ethan ended up putting the pack on a couple of government watch lists for a while after getting some of our gifts, mostly mine, through some contacts he discovered on the dark web. After explaining the situation at the beach and how I fucked up, I tell Ric about what I thought was going to happen.

"Anyways, it took me the whole night and most of the next day to come to terms with the whole mate thing. My plan upon coming back to the house was to see you and Ethan together once more so I could give up on my feelings once and for all. Then, I was going to go beg my mate to give me a chance to get over my human feelings. But you went and fucked everything up."

I explain how the month with Ethan fucked with my head even more. "I fell more and more in love yet again while I deluded myself into believing he was done with you. I redoubled my efforts to find a way to break the bonds of fate so I could free us *both*, convinced myself we would be happier together."

Ric cringes when I tell him how Josh caught a set of stray thoughts near the cabin and it made things even worse between us. And then came the icing on the cake, "Then, after chasing down the fae and everything, Ethan ran straight to *you* at that dirty ass motel in Georgia. He saw *me* over the railing and his face fell."

I can't help but let the tears fall. It's enough of a struggle to keep my voice from breaking along with my heart.

"His face fucking fell when he saw me, Ric. Then, he saw you and he was alive in a way I hadn't seen since Christmas morning. That was the moment I knew I had lost everything. I lost my mate, my best friend, and the love of my life in one instant."

My Alpha hands me a glass of whiskey. The look he gives me tells me we are still good. He isn't going to punish me. Apparently I'm doing enough of that on my own. If only spilling my guts like this could fix things with my mate...

13

JOSH

"You *WILL* be attending the party tomorrow, Joshua."

Uncle Edward's voice cuts through the thoughts running rampant in my head. I have spent the last two months doing anything I possibly could to avoid coming back home, well to his house anyway. I have been struggling, trying to figure out a way to make my heart beat again. I know that I need to meet with my mate to rectify this situation, officially reject one another, but I am a fucking coward.

I don't want to have that finality. The proof that I am a failure, that even the fates can't force someone to want me over my cousin.

"I'm not sure I'll make it in time, Uncle," I tell him while trying to calculate how far away I can get to justify the lie. Maybe my second cousins in Canada will let me cross over the border to hide?

"No excuses, Joshua," my king tells me. "There is nowhere in our territory that you cannot reach home within a day."

He doesn't give me a chance to refuse before he disconnects the call.

As I pull my phone away from my ear, I grimace at the wallpaper on my home screen. I never changed it from the photo of my family from my sixteenth birthday. My Mama has her arms around my waist, even though her head barely reaches my shoulders, and all of my siblings are behind us, leaning over. Dad took the photo or else he would have been in it as well. Even with me being the shortest of my siblings, Mama looked like our little sister that day, not like our mother. We were all laughing in that moment, pure joy reflecting in all of our eyes.

There haven't been many days since then that I've had reason to laugh.

Chase clearing his throat from the doorway startles me. "The king has ordered us back. The car is packed and we will be back in South Carolina by dawn."

Staring at my phone again, I change the wallpaper to a random color. If I am going to somehow make it through the next seventy or eighty years, I am going to have to learn to shut off the pain somehow. I have to cut everyone out, especially those I might hurt by not being able to love them anymore.

14

JOSH

<u>August</u>

> **Asshole Mate:**
> What do I have to do to prove it to you?

The asshat that fate saddled with me, Maximillian, has been hounding me since the party to try and weasel his way into my life. I understand the sentiment, but not the reasoning. At the party a couple months ago, my heart started to beat as soon as I was in the same room as him. I asked Ethan about him but ran away before we could speak.

I wanted to test the newly pumping blood to see if I could get some action, anything to take my mind off the pain of his rejection. Unfortunately, as soon as I left the Alpha's house, my heart stopped again. I tested it again on the fourth of July. I was hiding at the edge of the property, watching their backyard gathering, and ended up with the same results. It seems my heart will only beat in the presence of my mate now.

How the fuck did Uncle Edward survive this? How did he overcome his dead heart? I know his beats now, but how? Is it because

Olivia died? As much as I want my heart to beat again, I don't want my mate to die.

> **Asshole Mate:**
> I want only you, my mate. Please give us a chance.

I snarl at my phone and throw it to the ground. It's easy to lie in a text message. Bad enough he stole my number from Ethan's phone, but he has been harassing me daily. If it wasn't for the fact that he is the head warrior for the Jameson pack, he probably would have tried to physically hunt me down by now. Ethan being pregnant has certainly been in my favor this time. I'm not ready to face my two-faced mate.

Joshua! We are needed to transport Ethan and his doctor-friend to the hospital. Get to Alaric and Ethan's house immediately!

My uncle reaches me through the mind speak seconds before the sound comes through on my phone to indicate a new message. I pick it up from the ground, wincing at the cracked screen. When I open the app, I see a notification that *Jack the Magnificent* has started a chat labeled:

BABIES ARE COMING!

I take the clue and race over to grab Shaun to get him to the hospital. I'll read the rest of the notifications later, once my baby cousins come safely into this world. It's bad enough Ethan is an omega and was put through so much more than most people even guessed at long before he was rescued. Then fate had to screw him over again by giving him *fucking triplets* to give birth to.

When I drop Shaun in the room, Ethan grabs my wrist from where he is on the elevated exam bed to stop me from leaving. The sterile smells of the disinfectant don't bother me, but the underlying scent of blood is everywhere in this building. My anxiety is ramping up, but when I look into my cousin's eyes, I see both fear and resolve.

Stay, Sully. Please? Ethan sends me a message through mind speak while his eyes are begging. *I don't know if I'm going to make it and I need someone strong enough to restrain Ric if he loses it. Grandpa Eddie won't be in any shape to do it.*

My cousin is begging me to keep his mate from going nuclear if he should die. This isn't fucking fair! Ethan is the bravest, most amazing guy that has probably ever existed in our family, and...

Fate can't be that fucking cruel.

I pull his hand from my wrist to grasp his in my own. Giving a small squeeze, I don't lie to him exactly. I just let him interpret my actions as agreement. It's enough to get him to calm down enough so that Shaun and the nurses are able to get everything ready for the delivery.

Hours later, Ethan is still suffering from the contractions, but we are all just waiting for his body to be fully ready. I heard that with women, it can take over twenty-four hours for the first birth sometimes. Shaun said omegas tend to take longer to get to full dilation or whatever, so I'm just chilling in the chair next to the bed listening to Ethan's description of the "Thanksgiving Meltopia" that took place in November. Anything that keeps me from focusing on my own fucked up life is perfect right about now.

"And the next day, Max took me Black Friday shopping," he tells me and my heart gives a half attempt at a beat, just from the mention of my mate. "Apparently, he got hit by a couple cars and got into a few fights. I never saw it though. He won't walk around the front of cars to this day because of it, according to Bast."

He chuckles while I feel a chill run through my body. My mate was seriously injured multiple times because of holiday shopping?! Next year, my cousin is taking his own fucking mate out for his jollies around the holidays. Maximillian is not going to be the one guarding Ethan anymore, not if I have any say in the matter.

"Where's Shaun?" Ethan breaks through my thoughts after a long moment of silence in the room. Actually, the silence is too heavy. I can't hear anyone or anything outside of this room. Even the scent of blood has disappeared.

Something hard comes into contact with the back of my head, and I lose consciousness for a little while. When I come to, I hear a voice that I have prayed every night never to hear again. The fucking psycho in charge of the lab is in the room with us!

Before I can jump him, another voice sounds out in the room. It is a woman's voice, and not one that I recognize. There were no women as far as the lab staff went. That's part of the reason so many of us were taken advantage of. The men were "fulfilling their needs" with the unwilling residents since they had to stay on site while they were on shift. Could this woman be a nurse here at the hospital?

Uncle Edward? We got a problem in here. Can you hear me?

I send a message out using the mind speak, hoping that we aren't in a completely different plane of existence. I have zero clue if our family ability will work across that kind of distance. I know I can't reach Pop-Pop in Australia from our territory on the east coast, but I can sometimes reach Mama and Dad in California if they're open.

Joshua? The door has vanished. Are you both alright?

Well, that is a loaded question. I send word back to him, letting him hear directly what is being said, but then the bitch in the room, who is not a nurse, but apparently the werewolves' precious Goddess, starts sharing memories with Ethan directly and I can't listen in. The mental shields that Shaun put on Ethan's mind to contain the pain from his contractions have managed to completely shut me out.

Opening up my eyes, I can see the bastard from the lab staring at Ethan's belly with lust. He wants the babies. That's all he's wanted from Ethan from the time my cousin started to produce slick as an omega. If I have any say in it, he's not leaving this room alive let alone with a baby.

The so-called Goddess has Ethan transfixed, but the asshat in the lab coat doesn't seem to care. He wraps his hands around my cousin's throat, and I'm forced to watch the blood vessels burst in his eyes while I fight against my own panic to move my body. Between hearing and seeing the man, my anxiety has reached an all-time high since I've been free. Every cell in my body is telling me to save myself.

But I *have* to save Ethan!

I grip my phone in my pocket, and the feel of it in my hand anchors me to the fact that I'm not in the lab. I can't be back there. If my phone is with me, I'm not there...

I throw the phone at the back of the fucker's head and smile when he collapses to the floor. I hope he's dead, but I know my luck isn't that good. Even if he's still breathing, at least something happened. I can now hear people outside of the door. I jump up to look at Ethan only to see his empty bloody eyes staring up at the ceiling. There's no heartbeat from him. He's not breathing!

Fuck!

I have to save him! I have to save Ethan!

I start CPR before the door even opens. I learned this in middle school and remember thinking it was so pointless as a vampire to know CPR. Maybe, if I paid enough attention back then, I could save him now.

Shaun pushes me aside and the scent of blood rips through the room. I glance over at Ethan and see that his doctor friend has cut him open to get the babies out.

Of course, Ethan is dead so this is the only way the babies could live.

Ethan is dead.

Blood is death.

Blood...

I'm thrown into memory and trapped by the blood. It's always the blood.

15

MAX

First thing I see when I come into the room is my favorite little dude lying on the table, eyes unseeing. His body... No... his corpse is shaking sporadically from the motions his best friend is taking to save his babies. Tears start stinging my eyes and I fight to keep them from falling.

Ethan will come back. He always does. His father's curse runs in him. He isn't gone. He can't be.

A scream from the floor breaks me out of my grief, sending my wolf to the forefront of our minds. Josh is there on the floor next to the exam table, rocking back and forth, staring at something only he can see. My mate is a broken mess because of whatever happened in this room.

Ethan is gone and my mate is a mess. And I don't know what to do about it.

"Someone get him out of here!" Shaun yells when Josh screams again, fighting off anyone who gets too close. "I need to move where he is!"

Chase looks to me after Josh slashes open his side with his claws. I pray that my instincts are right as I reach for my mate. Hell, even if he covers me with scars, I will do anything in my power to relieve him of this agony he is in. When I reach him, I manage to scoop the smaller man into my arms and rush out the door.

I finally let my tears fall when I feel the steel bands of his arms wrap around me, holding on like I am his only anchor. He didn't push me away or fight me, and that is something I am profoundly grateful for.

While I hold and rock Josh in the backseat, Chase drives us back to their apartment just outside of the shopping district in town using the car he came in hours ago. The older vampire explains to me on the short drive that Josh still has some issues from his time in the lab that he doesn't want his family to know about while he works through them. That's why they live outside the estate, away from the other vampires. He says there's a lot more to it, but that Josh will need to explain.

It takes a few hours after I settle in at the apartment for Josh to completely come back to reality. Chase has already assured me this is a normal thing for my mate. I'm already on my second cup of coffee when I see the light returning to his eyes. His grip tightens briefly on my shoulders before he pulls his arms to his chest, folding in on himself again.

"Don't shut me out, Little One," I whisper, pressing a kiss to the top of his head, his chocolate curls tickling my nose. "Let me in. Let me take care of you."

He sniffles as if he has been crying, but there have been no tears this entire time. He looks so small and delicate right now that I can't help but treat him like a boy, *my* boy. He is mine in a way that Ethan never was or could be. The caregiver, the Daddy, in me loves this and craves this, although I wish it was not at the expense of his happiness.

"I'm not little," Josh pouts as he looks up at me. "I'm bigger than my Mama."

"Alright, Cutie." I can't stop my chuckle from escaping while I hug him a bit tighter, relishing the fact that he is perfect for me after all. "Will you talk to me? Tell me what happened back there?"

I feel a shiver run through him as he pulls himself together. There is a visible transition from the boy in my arms to the man who is now pacing in front of me. It started with the straightening of his posture, and then he pushed himself off my lap to start the back and forth across the room. Every third or fourth pass, he looks at me with confusion or contemplation, but it takes a while for him to start talking.

"I don't know how much my cousin has shared of his time in that place," he says when he stops in front of the window, staring at the curtains as if they were open and he could see the night sky. "Even I don't know all of the horrors he faced because he and I are ultimately too scientifically different. Since he was an omega, their focus for him was more about how a male body could even get pregnant, let alone carry a baby. They focused a lot on his reproductive system from what I picked up, especially after he *matured*."

He turns his head to the side, not exactly looking at me, but it's obvious he wants to know my reaction. It is important to him to know how much I know.

"I know a little of what Little Dude suffered in there," I tell him, unable to hide the disgust in my voice. "His nightmares have been pretty vivid throughout the pregnancy. Everyone in the house has seen and experienced exactly what Ethan has thanks to his memories leaking through in his dreams. Well, everyone except Jackie cuz Shaun warded his room to all hell to keep everything out. Some of my warriors took to napping on the floor in there just to be able to function with the bombardment.

"I sometimes wonder how in the hell he is still relatively sane after all that he went through," I whisper at the end.

Josh turns back to the curtains and hangs his head. I almost don't hear it when he whispers, "It would have been easier if we had died there."

16

JOSH

I'm glad I'm facing away so that Max can't see the corner of my lips turn up ever so slightly at the sound of his responding growl. Part of me, a rather large part I hate to admit, is unsure if the growl is for my sake or my cousin's. I shouldn't care. We both suffered so very much in there.

"It might be *easier* to show you my memories," I say, turning back towards the couch where he has been sitting for at least as long as I've been aware. I don't remember much between the blood and waking up on his lap. It was *really* fucking nice being in his arms. "But I can't guarantee I won't get stuck in them if I relive them. I've been trapped once already today and to be honest, I'm too chicken shit to face them like that again so soon."

The shame of my cowardice makes me lower my head, but seconds later his arm wraps around me and my face is buried in his chest. Our height difference means my head seems to tuck perfectly under his chin like this, and the scratch of his stubble on my scalp feels oddly soothing. He has one hand rubbing soothing circles on my back, while the other is holding my head securely in place, making me feel safe for the first time since I was dumb enough to get caught all those years ago.

"You can tell me as little or as much as you want. Whenever you are ready," Max says. "All I want is to take care of you and make you mine. Your safety, your comfort, your joy, and your fear... they are mine now, so let me have them."

The wall I had built up against this man crumbles to dust with his claim on me. Horrible ugly sobs escape despite trying to hold them inside. Even with all of the night terrors and panic attacks, I haven't ever let anyone see how broken I have been emotionally. There is something about Max that allows me to let go, to release the pain. Something about having him here has allowed me to connect with a part of me that has been locked away since my life was taken from me at sixteen, when Ethan was taken. I was locked up emotionally long before I was captured.

After a while, my body finally relaxes and the choking sobs start to slow. Through all of that time, Max just stood there and held me, letting me release all of the pain that I kept trapped inside. When I think he's going to release his hold on me, I let out a squeak as the big oaf scoops me up bridal style and carries me to my bedroom. I don't know how he knows which room is mine. Hell, I don't even know how he is here. No one but Chase knows about this place.

"Where's Chase?" I ask when Max lays me down on the bed. "He's not supposed to leave me alone, especially when I'm... *incoherent.*"

"Your bodyguard rightly decided you were safe with your mate and decided to get his wounds treated before they scar. You really did a number on him at the hospital."

Scar? I feel my eyes widen in response to his statement. Just how badly did I hurt my best friend this time?

Oh, Shit! How much did everyone see? Uncle Edward will send me back home to California if he figures out how fucked up I am now. And I can't hide a damn thing from Mama if she sees me in person. I'm already a disappointment to Dad and my brothers.

I try to jump out of the bed, but Max pushes me back down with gentle hands on my shoulders. My breathing is going erratic again, but I have to do something to fix this. My family can't find out about this. Hell, the supernaturals in the whole fucking kingdom can't find out! A regent can't be broken, not if they want to survive and keep the peace.

"Easy, Little One," Max murmurs to me. "Breathe with me. In for four and hold for four. One. Two. Three. Four..."

I follow his breathing instructions and feel my body start to relax. The feeling of panic is still clawing at my brain, but my eyes won't leave his. They are pools of infinite darkness, pulling me under his spell. In this light, I can't make out the exact color, but they are dark enough to look black. Combined with the sinfully bronzed tone of his skin, there's no denying that my fated mate is gorgeous. I just wish what I could give him in return was the same. I'm nothing but a scrawny, pale freak.

"You're gonna have to stop looking at me like that, Cutie, or I won't be able to hold back."

I don't really want him to hold back. I want to feel wanted for more than my position. I want to feel *something* more than fear and shame. I want *him*.

So, I reach up to pull him down on top of me using my own strength, crushing my lips to his. This isn't my first kiss, but it quickly makes all the previous attempts nonexistent. Nothing else compares as my body comes alive in ways I could never imagine. Nerve endings that I never knew existed start to wake up, sending sparks dancing across my body wherever we touch. The sounds and smells around me become more vibrant, echoing through me as if they are physical sensations.

I start to pull away when I remember that my mate still needs to breathe, but Max drops his full weight on top of me on the bed. My gasp of surprise gives him the opening to thrust his tongue into my mouth, and I think I'm in heaven. I've tasted other men, but every memory fades in comparison to this moment. Max is like triple chocolate cake with a dark chocolate ganache – so decadent that I want to savor it while at the same time have it as often as I can. I'm going to be addicted if this keeps up.

So sweet.

I can hear him in my mind and it causes my confidence to grow, along with another part of me. His soft growls spur me on. I take the kiss deeper, my hands gripping his shoulders hard enough that I'm sure he will bruise even with his wolf healing him.

Worth it, a deeper voice growls in my head. Did I just hear his wolf?

I hear Max grunt in a way that I take for encouragement, but then I freeze. I smell blood. I pull my hands back with a whimper. Noticing the change in me, Max slides off to my side, giving me a questioning look. I'm not sure how much he is able to read on my face, but he begins to run his hand down my body to soothe me. It's not enough because the only thing I can see before the world starts to gray around me is the sticky red substance coating my fingertips.

17

MAX

Looking at the beautiful boy that fate has given me, I can't help feeling immense satisfaction that he's bled me. I hope to wear the scars of his claws digging into my shoulders and back for the rest of our lives. My soul craves the physical manifestation of our time together. Our connection is unbelievable and nothing like what I could have ever imagined. The love I felt for Ethan is nothing like what I feel for my mate.

Tearing my eyes away from Josh's gorgeous body, I glance at his eyes and notice there is something wrong. His eyes are going vacant and he has stopped breathing. His heart beat is racing, but he isn't taking in any air. Having seen enough of them with Ethan over the last year, I know it's a panic attack, but I can't see any immediate reason for what might have caused it, unless he was used the same way Ethan was in that lab and I just put him back there...

"Baby?" I grab the sides of his face and turn him to me. I see no recognition. I move my hands to his shoulders and give him a little shake, but instead of looking at me, his gaze drops to his hands. When I look at them, I see his fingertips are red with my blood. The feeling of pride I had been feeling is leeched away by the fear taking hold.

On one hand, I am extremely proud to have had my mate mark

me by drawing blood. Blood is fucking sacred to his species way of life. Blood is literally life to vampires. No wolf would ever let a vampire draw their blood unless there is a huge amount of trust between them. The fact that my wolf allowed it and relishes it is testament to how much we trust and need our mate.

On the other hand, I'm afraid of what it means that my blood has sent Josh back into his catatonic state. Was it just the blood? Was it being intimate? I don't know and that is fucking terrifying.

Did they take him in that place? My wolf growls in my head, giving voice to the question I have been actively trying to ignore. I've seen what Ethan suffered in the lab. I am fully aware of how it feels to have that choice taken from you, to be powerless against another's sexual advances.

I pull off my torn and already blood-stained shirt to wipe Josh's hands clean. I know the small wounds on my back have already stopped bleeding, so I focus on cleaning him up. Once I have his hands as clean as I can without soap and water, I pull my mate into my side to hold him close. My own memories are fighting to come through, but I keep my mental walls up. Josh needs me to be the warrior, his rock and protector. He doesn't need to know about my mother.

I need to figure out how I'm going to handle it if he was violated in that place. I won't put him through the trauma of bottoming if he's suffered the same as Ethan while he was trapped there. Unfortunately for me, that means I need to face my own issues with it. It might be the only way to help my mate heal.

Twenty Years Ago

She put me in the closet like she always does when she has her grown-up time, but now there's a man opening the door. Did she forget to lock it again? Last time this happened, Mommy got really mad at the man and beat him up and sent him away. That's why I called out for her. She always saves me. Why isn't she answering me?

"You're sure he's never been touched?" the man asks someone behind him. I'm scared. What does he mean touched? Mommy gives me hugs all the time.

"No, the brat hasn't been touched before. Use the bathroom if you must, but I will charge extra if I have to do cleanup."

Wait? That is Mommy's voice...

"Come on, son," the man says gently as he pulls me up into his arms. He is gentle which is weird for me. I've never had a man be with me. Usually, Mommy's friends look and act really mean to me when they see me. This man looks nice, and he smells a lot better than most of the grownups that come into our house.

The nice man carries me to the bathroom and starts to take off my clothes. I love bath time! Maybe he'll let me play in the water. Mommy doesn't let me anymore. She says now that I'm almost seven, I need to be a big boy and take showers. Baths are for babies, she says. But the nice man looks like he's going to help me sneak having one.

"Let's play a little bit, sweet boy," he says as he gives me a tickle, making me giggle. I've never met a grownup that likes to be silly like this.

I feel a bit funny when he starts taking off his clothes. This is strange. Mommy never got naked to give me a bath.

"You are so sweet."

I don't know what's happening. The man is touching me and making funny noises. He keeps giving me kisses everywhere. Wait... Why is he kissing there? That's where my pee comes out!

"Mommy!"

I try to get to the door, to get away from the man. I was wrong. He's not nice. He's creepy and scary. I don't wanna do this!

"Mommy! Help!"

The man puts his big hand over my mouth and I feel pain in my whole body when he does something to my bum. I'm being torn apart! Please, Mommy, save me!

I cry and cry, but he doesn't stop. The pain doesn't stop. After a long time, the man eventually leaves me in the tub, turning on the shower. I watch the pink water go down the drain until it turns clear. I didn't even get my bath...

Fifteen Years Ago

The Alpha is visiting our house again, so I snuck out. I actually prefer it when he is there because it means there's no risk of anything happening to me except getting yelled at. I've spent the last five years as a surrogate for my mother whenever she is too drunk or high to be a good fuck for her clients, or as the first choice for a sect of them. Very few of the men who come over are actually repulsed by the thought of touching a boy. This pack is rotten to its core.

Even with it being after dark, I wander through the trees with no destination in mind. The only thing I'm certain of is that I don't want to be home. I wish there was somewhere I could go, someone who would love me.

A sound behind me makes me jump and I struggle to resist the urge to run. I am a wolf! I might not have him yet, but it doesn't change the fact that I am the predator in these woods. No rabbit is going to send me running!

"Oh sweet boy, I guess I get a special treat today."

My body freezes in response to that voice. This man has held the starring role in my nightmares for five years. He is the one who broke my body the first time. He is the one who KEEPS breaking me over and over and over again. Mother says he is responsible for keeping our lights on so I need to keep him happy. I don't want him happy. I want him gone.

"You can't touch me here," I say in a whisper. I meant to shout it, maybe alert someone else, but my voice is always stuck around him. He always finds ways to keep me quiet. I don't like them.

"Of course not here, but I can't pass up this opportunity," he replies as he throws me over his shoulder. He changes directions and we're heading toward the nicer houses in the pack, where me and Mother could never imagine living. If he gets me to his home, he will never let me leave. I'll have to deal with what he does every day and Mother won't even get the money for it. What will happen to her without that money?

"Let me go!" I squeak out, beating my fists on his back. He lands a smack on my behind hard enough to make me gasp. Mother has had to remind him a few times that I'm not old enough to take full force, whatever

that means. I feel so much pain in my leg and wonder if he managed to break the bone. I'm seeing stars. It hurts so badly as my body bounces on his shulder with each step he takes.

Too soon, I notice he is walking on pavement instead of the forest floor. I know it's over for me. This is it. This is my end. I'll have to suffer over and over until I die. How does Mother do it?

"Drop the kid, Jonas," a woman's voice growls from in front of the man. "This is your only warning."

My nightmare man tosses me down on the concrete and I curl up in a ball, whimpering at the additional pain from the impact. I really hope that the lady was smart enough to bring a man to help her. This man is too strong and too well connected in the pack. He is head of the Alpha's warriors. There is no one above the Alpha and the Beta in a pack for power and influence, but the head warrior is strongest wolf in the pack physically.

"Anna, you should know your place by now. I'm sure Richard won't mind me teaching you a lesson in respecting your superiors," the man growls before I glimpse the flash of fur when he transforms. As a wolf, he's a muddy brown color. I pray that my wolf will look nothing like him.

I'm always afraid that I'll find out one of the men who hurts me is my dad...

"Your death it is, Jonas," the woman, Anna, sighs before the sounds of snarls and growls break the silence of the night. I can't stop the whimpers that escape as my body trembles in terror.

When a cold, wet snout touches the back of my neck, I scream and wet myself. This lady tried to help me and now she's dead and I'm going to die, only more slowly and painfully...

"Shhhh..." the lady's voice surprises me as I flinch away from her gentle touch. "I'm going to help you, boy. He won't hurt you ever again. He won't hurt anyone ever again..."

18

JOSH

I blink away the tears that want to fall for the man in my bed. Shortly after he wiped away the blood on my hands, I broke free of my own memories, only to fall into his. I can't believe this amazing and strong man suffered so much for so long and no one knew. Well, the lady knew, whoever she is.

Did she kill him? I can't stop the thought from going out and I feel Max tense beneath me.

"Did you see all of that, Little One?" he asks me, tension recognizable in his voice. "I understand if you don't want to be intimate with me because of your time away, but I'm willing to try... *receiving*... for you. If you need me to, I will do anything for you."

I shake my head and sit up in the bed next to him. While he shifts himself to sit next to me, I make an attempt to explain what happened with me and what I saw during my captivity.

"I've never been forced," I tell him as he tucks me into his side. I lay my head on his shoulder, staring out into my dark bedroom. "At least, not receiving. They tried to force me to top some of the other captives, but I refused. Knowing now what the consequences were for some of them, I almost wish I hadn't.

"The first year or so in there was just vivisection and them withholding blood to keep me weaker. I likely would have died if I didn't have special abilities from my mother's side of the family. The idiots put me in a room with a skylight. I was sixteen and my healing would have been too slow to keep up with the sunburn and the vivisection without it. They thought they were starving me, and I played along. I was weak enough to pull it off, since all the energy I consumed went to healing and keeping my heart beating.

"Things got both better and worse when they started the battle royale in the basement. That's when I first met Ethan. He had already befriended a fae girl, Celeste, and the two of them brought me into their little circle. The mind link was something I used with them, and we kept each other sane during the matches. I think they wanted us, me especially, to go insane with the blood and fighting, but instead we bonded.

"After another year or so of the fighting, I was brought back into the lab for more experiments. They would bleed another captive in front of me, but not let me feed. It wasn't that bad for me, but I had to watch over and over as they would slice up other victims in front of me, trying to force me to feed from them or fuck them. At this point, they were moving their interest to hybrids between the species more than our biology itself."

I glance up at Max to see his jaw tightly clenched as he stares at the ceiling. A tear falls from his eye, but if I hadn't been looking, I wouldn't have known he is so affected. Is it wrong that it gives me some warm and fuzzy feelings that he's upset over this?

Oh, maybe it's just because of Ethan. That makes more sense.

I let a shiver run through my body to shake myself out of those thoughts. I want to trust that my mate is here with me because he wants me, not because he can't have my cousin. I *need* to trust him.

"That's about the time I put the dots together and realized Ethan was actually my cousin who we all thought was dead. When he turned sixteen, his vampire side fully awakened and I felt the family bond the next time he talked to me using mind speak. At that point, I needed to get him out of there. It became more than just rescuing a friend or helping out a lonely wolf boy. It was the mission I was raised for.

"Ethan's safety has always trumped my own," I explain offhandedly, "as it should be since he is the legitimate heir of Uncle Edward. I've only ever been a replacement."

"You're not a replacement," Max growls out before kissing the top of my head. "Not for the vampires, not for your family, and especially not for me. You are my universe, my heart, my life... my one and *only* boy."

I can't hide my smile when I shiver again, this time for a completely different reason. My soul is hungry for this man, but true hunger wins out when my stomach decides to growl audibly. Max chuckles and pats the offensive area of my body before sliding away and off the bed.

"Let's get some food in you. We can leave the heavy topics for later. I want to get back to the hospital to check on everyone, meet my godkid," he says as he stretches. I only just now noticed he's naked from the waist up. There are ten scabs across the top of his back and shoulders and I gasp. My claws did that...

"Badges of honor, babe," he smirks over his shoulder before picking up his shirt from the floor. There are bloodstains all over it and I cringe. "You think this can be saved or maybe your roomie has a shirt I can borrow? Yours will never fit me."

I force a chuckle that I don't really feel as I climb out of the bed. I need to burn that shirt before the smell triggers me again. I take a deep breath of the clean hallway air before I reach the door to Chase's room. He opens up before I even knock and hands me a t-shirt with a smile.

"It's good to see the light in your eyes, Josh," he tells me, leaning on the door frame. "You need someone like him, someone who is tough enough to carry your past but soft enough to keep you safe. He won't hold you back. He will help you soar if you let him in."

Chase laughs and pushes my dazed ass back down the hallway toward the kitchen where a shirtless Max is cooking something that smells divine.

I'll go burn his shirt for you, my friend sends to me as he turns back to the hallway. *Although if this is the view that makes you smile like that, I might have to preemptively burn them all just to be safe.*

76

I know the stupid sappy smile is still on my face all through our meal and the short drive back to the hospital. It doesn't fade until walking into the room to see Ethan in the hospital bed. Or rather, his corpse on the bed. My cousin is dead, and it is all my fault for being a fucking coward.

19

MAX

<u>September</u>

Of course, Ethan decided I was to be the godfather to the kid who can't seem to stop shitting on himself. Not gonna lie, Alec is adorable as fuck. But I've gotten way too used to changing dirty diapers and cleaning up blowouts over the last two weeks. Granted, most of that time was while Little Dude was still technically dead, but I was getting the literal shit end of the stick here.

Ric wasn't cool with having my mate staying at the house with his whole vampire complex thing, so I've been sneaking out to see him when the babies are asleep. It has been two exhausting weeks of balancing my time between my newborn godson and my distraught mate. Now, that Little Dude is awake, I'm super excited to let Josh know.

> **Me:**
> Guess who is awake now?

> U need 2 get over here for some baby cuddles

Ric is being a little bitch about something already. It has barely been twenty minutes since Ethan woke up, and he's sulking. Shaun and Jack are helping Ethan to get the babies fed while I wait for Josh to show up. Considering how stressed the Little Dude is with just coming back from the dead and all, I grab his favorite bluebird sippy cup and fill it with chocolate milk. He can't fully go little right now with needing to take care of the babies, but at least this should help since his mate is being a humongous dickhead.

I trade Ethan the sippy for the baby and start burping Alec. Me and my godson have gotten very well acquainted over the last couple weeks. He only pukes on me half the time now, unlike his brother Zander. That boy is a puke machine if anyone other than Jack tries to burp him. In fact, Zander reminds me a lot of Jackie as a baby.

Eight Years Ago

"You're not going to hurt him, Max," Alpha Mate Anna says as she hands me the warm bottle. "Babies are more resilient than you think, and he'll only pick up on your tension and start screaming if you're tense."

I take the bottle in my left hand and let Miss Anna reposition her baby in my arms. I don't know how she figured it out, but she ambushed me this morning on the way out of the pack. I lost the only person I truly cared about in this pack, the only one who needs me... needed me. I got my mother settled, and I came back to the new territory just long enough to make sure Miss Anna made it through her pregnancy. She delivered a healthy baby, and there wasn't supposed to be anything holding me here.

Looking down at the tiny little human in my arms, I know I can't leave now. I have to make sure nothing happens to this little guy. The darkness in this pack that devours me every day, that killed Ethan... it will never touch this baby. Glancing up at Miss Anna, I can see in her eyes that she understands. She gave me a reason to stay, a reason to not completely close off my heart.

"Fate has a plan for you, son," she whispers, placing a hand on my shoulder. "Keep my son safe. Both of them if you can, but Ric might be too far gone without his mate. You have to protect Jack, even from his family if it comes down to it."

I look at her in surprise. What is she talking about? I know that Alpha Dick is an asshole to others, but he wouldn't really hurt his own kid, right?

"Aaron will train you," she says focusing her attention out of the window. "If you think my eldest is not a good enough guardian for him, promise me you'll take him away. Take him to my father's pack in Michigan. Please, Max. You are the only one I can trust in this pack to see the evil outside of my brother."

Swallowing heavily, I nod when she meets my eyes. This is a lot to put on a nineteen-year-old, but I will do it. If there had been somewhere to take Ethan, I would have escaped with him years ago to save him. Even if I had nowhere to go, I won't make the same mistake with Jack.

"Jack will never suffer from the evils in this pack or this world. Not while I live," I tell her with all the authority I can muster. The silence after my statement is heavy, almost like I used an Alpha's authority to swear an oath. But I'm just a bastard, not an Alpha. My father was a no name beta warrior who abandoned his mate when she got pregnant.

The sound of my phone alerting me to a text message pulls me from my memory. I don't even get a chance to read it before the shutters are slamming shut on the house. Why the fuck did the Alpha activate them?

Ethan runs out of the kitchen, clutching a screeching Tessa to his chest. I nod for Zach, one of the beta wolves that has become a part of our central group, to go after him to take the baby. I balance a screaming Alec against my chest enough to pull out my phone. Sure enough, there is a text from the asshole.

Ric-Roll:
Keep them safe.

Voice in head. Not me.

Don't trust me.

Love him.

Love them.

Don't trust me

When I reach the hallway, Ethan has handed Tessa over to her Uncle Jack, so I hand Alec over to Zach, who was only bringing his nephew over to hang with Jackie. Looking at my phone, I realize Ric has activated the full security protocol when I notice there are no bars showing at all. Where the screen would show bars or 5G or LTE, it now reads "No Service". The jammers that I never got around to disabling or locating their controls seem to be working just fine.

"No service with the shutters down, but a message came through right before we got sealed in," I reluctantly tell the group gathered in the hallway. Glancing over Ethan's shoulder, I see that Josh made it inside before we got sealed in and I'm not sure if I'm glad of that. I give my mate direct eye contact as I continue. "We're stuck here for the time being. Just waiting on our Alpha to take care of something."

I want to reassure my mate, but Ethan demands my phone. Technically without Ric here, he *is* most senior ranking wolf and I have to listen to him. I hand it over and look at Josh with an apology in my eyes. We've had many conversations over the last two weeks, and I know he doesn't do well with confinement. I feel guilty because my eagerness to see my mate has trapped him in here.

Before I can say anything more, Ethan is gone from in front of me. My mate is gone as well. Fucking vamp speed!

I hear a commotion coming from the Beta suite of rooms and race there to find my mate restraining his cousin. Before I can even ask what is going on, Ethan drops to the floor in tears. I rush to check him over, trying to ignore the flash of pain that moves across Josh's face. I wish I could explain to him that it's not love, but duty that makes me check on Ethan here. At least, it's not romantic love. If I had to label it, Ethan is my closest friend, my chosen family. He is my little brother.

My Alpha Mate questions me about *his* dickhead mate and then calls for war via a mental blast to the whole pack. I leave the two boys on the floor of the suite while I head to my own suite upstairs to start preparing what I can. My foot is on the first step when I hear my mate, "HURLEY?! Who's a Hurley?!"

20

JOSH

My cousin is a fucking witch who can control the dead. Holy fucking shit...

Well, part witch anyways.

Doesn't matter.

Uncle Edward? I send out a call to him while Ethan is playing switchboard for the war council.

I can feel the annoyance when he responds, *I do not have time for this Joshua. There are things happening that are more important than your adolescent issues.*

Are you fucking kidding me?!

Is that really how you see me contacting you right now? As a teenager just bothering you to complain?

I'm seething and am not surprised when he dismisses me again with his fucking pretentious, holier than thou, you're too young to know anything bullshit: *I have bigger issues right now than whatever drama is happening with you. When we next see each other, I'm going to reevaluate whether or not you are ready to be my successor or if I need to select from one of your siblings. I do not have time for your juvenile grievances today!*

He breaks off the communication and throws a wall up between us. Why is it so difficult for anyone to just listen to me? What more do I have to do to earn his respect?

He thinks taking away the successorship is a punishment. Oh, fuck it would be a blessing for me, but it would make Dad and Mama upset. I don't want to cause problems in the family. I don't want to be sent home — not now that I've started making a real connection here.

I see Zach and the younger boys in the living room with the babies, so I turn away. I don't want to see them, or rather, I don't want them to see me. I can't go outside. I can't go to Max because he will know immediately something is wrong.

I wander through the house to try and find an empty room, just in case I blow. The panic at being locked in notches higher and higher with each shuttered window I pass.

When I come to the end of the upstairs hall, I am surprised to find my cousin sitting on the floor of his playroom arranging his stuffies in battle configurations. My brain supplies the image of Dad, Uncle Patrick, Uncle Reynaldo, and Uncle Edward trying to follow along with the Stuffie Army and can't stop the smile from breaking over my face. Giving the door a soft knock, I think it's time I talk to my cousin in depth for the first time since we first discovered each other outside of hell.

Sitting in the rocking chair, I give Ethan a crash course on vampires and abilities, and he gets it so much quicker than most. We're not dead, not really. But we're not alive. We are something outside of life, and the Hurley family of witches are necromancers of the highest caliber. It's rumored they can control anything that is dead or undead, like vampires. That's why they were supposed to be wiped out. In fact, Uncle Edward was supposed to have done the deed decades ago based on the words of some seer or something.

"My dad told me that my uncle killed the last of them over sixty years ago, but if you're a Hurley descendant then they missed one," I tell him. "Do you know if it was through your mom or your dad?"

Ethan hedges my question, and instead blows my mind with his response. I leap up from the rocking chair in shock, but can't seem to control my laughter.

"His *MATE* was a Hurley?!," I gasp out and proceed to fall to my ass in laughter. "Dad is *never* gonna let him live this down."

When I ask about Connor, his adoptive brother, Ethan growls protectively but I wave it off. I'm still riding the high of knowing my uncle fucked up and I can finally make *him* feel like shit for screwing up. He needs a reality check.

"So anyway, back on track," I say as I scoot over to my cousin, picking up a stuffed Cthulhu to hold, "Do you know if that lying goddess bitch had anyone else in your family swear loyalty to her aside from you and your fucked up deal?"

He answers no at first but then he looks at me like the virgin chick facing the killer in a horror movie. I almost laugh but then he races out of the room. I chase after him, but I don't notice quickly enough that we're in the kitchen and I'm only in my socks. Ethan stops suddenly, and my momentum is about to make me crash hard into the island. I'm slipping along the linoleum, arm flailing, when my mate steps into my path. I collide with Max and then darkness.

21

JOSH

Joshua! What the hell is wrong with you?

Groaning, I push myself up. When did I fall asleep? I hear another groan from underneath me and I'm surprised to see Max there, rubbing his palm over the back of his head.

Looking around, I notice we're on the floor of Ethan's kitchen. It takes a few seconds for what happened to come back to me, and I can't help feeling embarrassed. What kind of vampire crashes and knocks themselves unconscious because they can't stop?

"You alright, Little One?" Max asks me, running his hands over my body to check for injuries. I bite my lip and nod. I like it when he calls me his Little One. Ethan might be "Little Dude" but I'm his "One." Yeah, it's petty, but I don't care. I like what I like.

Joshua!

I sigh and stand up, giving my mate a hand up as well before I answer my uncle. I don't know what the fuck his problem is right now, but he can wait. He didn't have time for me before, so he can learn some fucking patience his own damn self.

Son? My dad's voice cuts into my mind. *Why aren't you answering Edward?*

Fuck my life. The asshole regent can't wait five fucking minutes for a response before running to tattle to my father. This is just great.

Now, I'll have to explain everything to Mama and Drea and everyone before I even know what is going on myself...

Hey, Dad. I send back to him, hoping he doesn't pick up on my mood. *I'm just coming around after an incident with a kitchen counter. You can tell Mama she was right all along that socks in the kitchen with vamp speed is a dangerous combination.*

I can feel his chuckle and it sends warmth through me. I miss my parents so very much. Almost like he can sense I need it, Max puts his arms around me and pulls me back into his chest, resting his chin on my head.

I'm not going to share that with your Mama or else we will never hear the end of it for the next hundred years. And I still enjoy wearing only my socks in the house, thank you very much.

I smile at the thought of my tiny five foot nothing Mama lording it over everyone that they need grippy socks or slippers at all times in the house, never shoes though. Shoes are absolutely not allowed inside my Mama's house, not if you value your existence.

Since I know you are alive now, please answer your uncle before he becomes the first ever vampire to blow an aneurysm. I love my big brother, but he needs the stick removed from his ass...

I don't think Dad meant for me to hear that last part, but I don't disagree. Uncle Edward is wound too fucking tight and if he's not careful, he's going to alienate everyone that matters.

"I have to contact the king," I sigh out loud and Max gives me a brief squeeze before dropping his hands. I turn to face him and wrap my arms around him this time, burying my face in his chest. It is a *very* nice chest. "I don't want to talk to him after how he treated me earlier. He treats me like garbage and I feel like it enough as it is. I don't need my family reinforcing it."

Max growls as he wraps his arms back around me. "No one has the right to treat you that way, not even the fucking vampire king. Say the word and we'll leave as soon as this crisis is over. I won't let him make you miserable."

I sniffle a bit into his shirt before I pull back with a smile. That was exactly what I needed to hear. Chase might be my best friend, but he is bound by vampire law, and that means he can't help me run if I want to. He is oathbound to report to his king. Maybe fate has it right by giving me a wolf for a mate after all.

Squaring my shoulders, I reach back out to my asshole uncle. *Sorry that I was unconscious and it inconvenienced you, my liege. What pray tell is so important you had to tattle to my father?*

His icy tone isn't a surprise considering the attitude I fed him, but his words make me laugh out loud: *Why did you not inform me we were dealing with a Hurley witch, boy? Do you think this is a game? This is life and death for your cousin's mate!*

Max gives me a questioning glance, but the encouraging smile he flashes takes my breath away. He gives me the courage to stand up to my king.

I was trying to inform you earlier when you cut me off and told me you didn't have time for my adolescent drama, your majesty. I send to him with minimal snark... alright there is quite a lot of snark. It's not often I get to say I told you so to the fucking king. *I don't think it's quite fair to hold me accountable for you cutting me off and not listening.*

This will be discussed later, Joshua, Uncle Edward's voice comes through colder than usual, but not angry anymore. *I will need to use you to keep informed on what is going on within that house since Esther seems to be able to sense when I am connected to Ethan and gains some strength from it. We need to keep her as weakened as possible to expel her from her host.*

Oh, shit! Teasing over. This is actually really bad. I didn't realize the Hurley witch we are dealing with is the bitch who abused the fuck out of Ethan as a child. I hurriedly agree to my uncle's request and start coordinating with Connor and Ethan and the others to figure out how to get everything situated.

Eventually, the decision is made that we need a changing of the guard to get Connor along with a few of the guards inside with Ethan and the triplets. The consensus was reached as well to let the non-fighters take refuge in the Heartstone Pack. I also offered some of our safe houses as back up locations, just in case the fighting spilled over to the other pack. I gave the locations to Zach so that he and his nephew would ultimately be safe. I don't know many others in this pack, but the elementary teacher has been kind to me the entire time I've known him.

"Can you go outside and update Chase while I hold down the phone lines?" I ask Max while everyone is gearing up for the switch. Ethan and Shaun are already heading for the office with the babies as I see Connor coming in the front. "He needs to know where you think the borders are vulnerable so that our people can be positioned properly and know who not to attack if they cross. I have called up some of my best people for this, not just the meatheads my uncle uses for show."

After a quick glance around the room, Max nods and gives me a quick peck on the cheek. If I drank blood to waste on blushing, it would be very obvious how I'm feeling right now. I feel a little bad for being happy right now with everything going on, but fuck it. I finally have someone who put me first and he kissed me!

Turning back to the room with the warriors, I get ready to start relaying instructions when the shutters slam shut on the house again. What the hell?

Sorry, Sully, Ethan's voice cuts into my head. *I need to save him. I know what to do now and can't have you guys stopping me. Keep my babies safe for me and I'll be back later.*

His connection cuts out, but I'm having a hard time keeping calm. With my rational brain, I don't blame him for going after his mate. If something like this was happening with Max, nothing in the universe could keep me away. But he *locked* me in the house with strangers. The only ones I've had any interaction with are Jack and Shaun, neither of which could stop me if I fall into a panic attack right now

Max?! I send out in desperation. *I don't want to hurt them but I can't be trapped in here. Please, get me out of here!*

I feel his concern and love, but it isn't enough. I'm struggling to hold on to myself as I feel my heart trying to pound out of my chest. I run up to Ethan's playroom and lock the door behind me. Grabbing a random stuffie, I curl up in the rocking chair and hope that the house opens back up before my mind breaks again.

22

MAX

I had just finished filling Chase in on what he needs to know when I feel Josh's fear. Turning back to the house, I see the shutters are closed again, and the reason is apparently gearing up to run off to play hero to his mate.

"What the fuck do you think you're doing?" I ask Ethan, honestly wondering how he could abandon those babies. "Does anyone know you're outside?"

He says he snuck out like that's not obvious. "...where you would be if you weren't so pigheaded about my cousin..."

I cough to cover my smirk. I guess he hasn't noticed the change between us yet.

But before I can really pay attention to whatever Little Dude is doing, my mate's panicked voice filters through my mind. I can't split my focus between them, so I spend as much time as I possibly can reassuring Josh that I will get inside as quickly as I possibly can. At some point, Ethan slips away, but right now my mate is more important.

Let me tell you a story, Little One. Would you like that? I send to him, hoping that I can distract him enough to calm him down. I hear a vaguely affirmative response, so I decide to run with it. It's time for my mate to understand my story and that *he* is the only one in my heart.

23

MAX

Once upon a time, there was a young boy who loved his mother very much. It was the two of them against the world, especially after her mother, the boy's grandma, went to heaven when the boy was very very little. His mother was the most beautiful woman in the world to him, but then again, he didn't know anything about the world yet. They were about as far from rich as people could get, but they were blessed with love. They were happy. Then, his mother was cursed with a sickness.

In the beginning, the boy cared for his mother, hoping to cure her sickness. Some days, she even seemed to be better, but eventually her curse would always catch up to her and change her back to evil.

As the boy grew older, more and more evil men would visit their home. Some of them shared the curse his mother had. Others wanted to use the boy or his mother for their own pleasure. She accepted them all because she needed money to feed her curse. The boy lost the beautiful woman he admired for so long. She stopped being a mother long before the boy grew to adulthood.

For years, the boy dreamed of his father rescuing him, but as far as he knew, he never met the man. He even hoped that the Alpha of the land might be his father. Because if the most powerful wolf was his father, surely he could fix his mother and save him from the evil of the curse. So, the boy saved every penny he could in order to pay a witch to check if the powerful wolf was his father.

The witch was not kind, but she was honest. She told him that his father was not part of this land and would not be coming to the boy's rescue. His father did not even know the boy existed. The boy would need to save himself.

More years passed, and the curse only grew worse. But the boy was bigger and could run and hide away better. When hiding from his mother, the boy was captured by one of the evil men, who was taking him back to his lair. The boy was in despair, knowing that this was the end for him. He fought as hard as he could against the evil man. Yet he was too weak, and the man broke the boy's leg to cease his struggles.

Suddenly, an angel appeared in the form of a pure white wolf. She saved the boy from the evil man and helped get the boy cleaned and healed up. From that day on, the boy knew he had to get stronger. His angel might have saved him that day, but he decided to never be in that position again. He would never NEED saving again.

Even more time passed as the boy grew into a young man. He made friends with the other boys, but they didn't understand the curse hanging over his head. They didn't understand the darkness around their pack. He watched as each of his schoolmates connected with their wolves, seeing the familial resemblances at the pack gatherings, seeds of resentment growing inside him.

His wolf was kind and patient with the young man leading up to his change. Typically, it is the role of the parents, especially the father, to be there for the first shift of a wolf. The coloring of a wolf is determined by the father so the boy had no idea what to expect. On the morning of his thirteenth birthday, the boy crept into the woods to welcome his wolf all alone. He had no one to help him through it, for the curse stole his family from him.

It was agony, but his wolf was kind and kept talking to him, encouraging him. After a while, another voice was in the woods with him, speaking words of comfort and praise. It was his angel. She had come for his shift. She saved him again, and his wolf showed his appreciation by taking her coloring upon himself. As far as the young man was concerned, he had no father. So, he decided his wolf should look like the only person to ever show him true kindness.

He spent hours staring at his wolf's reflection in the little pond. At one point, his angel changed into her wolf form herself, and he allowed himself to imagine that she was his family, that SHE was really his mother, and not that cursed woman back at the house. Unfortunately, his angel had to leave to go home to her own boy, who never knew how blessed he truly was while our young man was living with evil.

More time passed and the young man grew both mentally and physically. He was no longer worried about the evil men around his mother. They could no longer touch him. The young man was growing up, looking forward to being able to set out on adventures, leaving the cursed woman behind. Fate had different ideas for him though.

One day, the young man saw a group of bullies attacking what he thought was a defenseless animal, so he chased them off. Only, it wasn't an animal, it was a much younger boy. This little boy reminded him of how powerless he used to be in the face of the curse, so he swore he would do whatever it took to protect this boy so he would never have to face the evil men like he did.

And for a few years, the young man was successful. He trained the little boy how to fight, how to use weapons; how to hide, and how to run. He taught the little boy all of the lessons he had to learn for himself. He even taught him how to recognize evil so that the boy might escape it, but it wasn't enough. Evil found the little boy and took him away.

The young man was now fully grown, but he was destroyed inside. He failed the little boy and intended to run away in his shame, but his angel saved him one last time. She called him over to her castle on the morning he was prepared to leave. He did not know what to expect, but she placed a baby in his arms, making him promise to protect this child even from his own family if necessary. The boy, now a man, could deny his angel nothing. She had saved him three times. He owed her much more than his own life.

Soon after the promise was made, his angel disappeared from this world, and the man's heart grew very dark. The only bright spot was her baby. Watching the baby grow, year after year, into a child of pure light and love brought a small measure of peace to the man, and a much larger dose of pain. This is what the little boy he failed should have been. This is what HE should have been.

The man lived in his shame for years, and when he was finally starting to forgive himself for his failures, the past caught up with him. The little boy he failed to save came back from the dead. Only, he wasn't dead at all. He had been taken by evil men, just like the man had. And the little boy had suffered the same way he had, except so much worse. The little boy had died over and over, mentally and physically, but there was no one to save him. He had no angel to come to his rescue.

The man, wracked with guilt, promised to be everything to the little boy. He swore his own happiness meant nothing if only he could heal the wounds that were ripped open in the boy from his failure.

But fate had other plans for the man. You see, that little boy already had his hero, but the man was blinded by his guilt. In his confusion, the man missed another little boy who needed him more. And the man needed this new boy like he needed air to breathe. In his haste to correct his failure, the man almost lost the most amazing boy in the universe.

Then, after some miscommunication, the man shared his first real kiss with this amazing boy and knew there will never be another more important to him in the entirety of existence. His only regret is that his angel will never get to meet the person who finally started to heal his heart.

24

JOSH

Tears are streaming down my face, but I don't care. I had no idea Max suffered like that. I mean, I saw a bit about the guy kidnapping him, but I can't imagine a mother selling her son like that. When I think of a mother, I picture my Mama. The thought of her doing anything to hurt one of her children is absolutely ridiculous.

I hear the shutters release, and I get up to unlock the door. I don't leave the room, though. I feel safe in here and if the shutters are up, that means the cell phones will work now. They don't need me if they can use phones, and for once, I'm glad to not be needed. I just want to cuddle and let everything else go right now.

When the door creaks open, I see my mate peek his head around the door to look around the room. He spots me curled up in the corner, surrounded by stuffies, and gives me a sad smile.

"You alright, Little One?" he asks and takes a seat next to me. He looks worried, but he doesn't need to be. Now that I know his story, I feel horrible for how I treated him.

"Cuddles?" I don't recognize my voice. It's too soft, too young. But it's the best I can get out. I feel way too vulnerable to speak any louder.

Max leans down to give me a kiss on my forehead before pulling me into his lap. "Always, Baby. You're my universe now."

25

MAX

The last twenty four hours have been like something out of a fucking movie! First, the Beta's dead mother possessed the Alpha, then jumped into her son and tried to kill the babies *and* Connor's mate, almost killing Connor in the process. After *that* nightmare was handled, then we had to battle the fucking pantheon of gods...

"Remind me to not piss off your cousin," I mumble to the vampire curled up under the covers on my bed. Josh's giggle is interrupted by his gigantic yawn and we both crack up in response.

Ethan saved the day in more than one way, but he is utterly fucking diabolical when it comes to punishments. Come to think of it, he always has been. Only now, he's got abilities that make him truly terrifying.

"I'm too tired to do anything to get on Ethan's bad side," Josh mutters into his pillow before looking up at me. "Plus, I think this time he knows he went too far. He is feeling guilty about it."

The goddess and her posse came for us with full force. We only repaid them in kind. All is fair in love and war and all that jazz.

I lay down next to my mate and pull him into my arms. It figures that the first time we are in bed together we are too exhausted to do anything other than sleep. I swallow a sigh when he turns to cuddle, using my chest as a pillow. The only thing that keeps running through my head is that this is how it should be every night, from now on.

The next two weeks are blissfully uneventful, with the exception of the triplets taking turns getting ear infections and keeping us all awake for days on end. I don't even blame Josh for heading back to his apartment after that first night. Between Ric's feelings about his species and three screaming newborns, I'm surprised more people haven't found other places to be. Hell, if it wasn't for the fact that our Beta is still being a dumbass and avoiding his mate, I would have followed Josh back to his place to escape baby-geddon. Even my wolf is getting fed up.

Mate not here, he sends to me every morning when I wake up. Like, yeah dude. Josh isn't here. I don't need the reminder when the scent of him fades from my mattress a little bit more each day. We still talk every morning before he turns in and I start my day, but it's not the same as that one glorious morning opening my eyes and seeing him in my arms.

"Earth to Maxi-pad?" Ethan's voice startles me, and I grab my coffee cup from the cabinet. I guess it was kind of obvious I was zoning out, standing there with the door wide open. Stepping back, Little Dude moves in front of me to reach up for his latest favorite mug. It has a giant glittery rainbow poop emoji on it and says "All That Glitters..." with a unicorn outline behind it. It was a gift from his father's mate, Lisa.

"So how's my cuz?" he asks as he pushes me out of the way to get to the coffee pods. "He's been keeping pretty mum about you two, but I know you won't skimp on the deets for me, right? Just cuz my brain doesn't like my body doing the sexy stuff, it doesn't mean I don't wanna hear about it. So, tea? Spill, please."

I'm kind of glad I hadn't gotten my coffee yet for that one because I would have spit it across the room.

"I don't need to know or think about your sex life, Little Dude," I tell him as he takes his full mug over to his seat at the island. Placing my cup under the spout and putting in a pod for my own cup of coffee, I turn to Ethan to unpack the rest of what he's said.

"As for the *deets*, there are none," I tell him, putting his latest creamer obsession on the island in front of him. He's on a salted caramel kick this week, and this is at least one that I will drink as well. "Josh and I haven't seen each other since your fiancé flipped out on him the day after the battle."

Ethan's smirk disappears and his body tenses up before he asks, "What did Ric do to Sully?"

The joking omega has disappeared and my Alpha Mate is the one asking. I tell Ethan everything I know about that morning, which isn't much. For a second, I'm really confused. I thought Ethan was aware of what happened because neither Josh nor Ric gave any indication that he was kept in the dark. Hell, I don't even know the specifics of what happened. I just know there was yelling and by the time I got to the kitchen that morning, Ric was the only one there. My mate texted a few minutes later to let me know he was at his apartment and he would call me later.

"I'll be having a talk with my mate," Ethan growls before taking another sip of his coffee. "*He* left me with the impression that my cousin had business to attend to and that's why I haven't been seeing him."

Before I can question him further, he hops down from his stool and stomps from the room, heading for the office. I really wouldn't want to be the Alpha right now, having to face off with an under-caffeinated and pissed off Ethan.

I want to know more for myself about what happened that morning, but Jack pounds down the stairs in the way only a nine-year-old can, reminding me that it's my turn to take him to school. I have to take him to his classes, and if we don't leave now, we're going to be late.

"Max-a-roni! Let's go!" he whisper yells from the hallway. I don't blame him for the attempt at being quiet considering all three babies are asleep at the same time for a change. Even with the warding and soundproofing on his room, they still manage to keep him up most nights.

I grab the keys to my motorcycle since they still haven't replaced the Navigator that was destroyed by the fae twins. Jackie does his happy dance when he sees me grab the child size helmet from the closet. He loves my bike, and I love making the little guy smile. He reminds me so much of his mother when he smiles.

"Let's go, Short Stack," I mumble and stuff the helmet on his head. He giggles as we head out the front door. Right before I start the bike, I hear yelling coming from the open window of the Alpha's office. I guess the soundproofing wards haven't been put back up yet. I know they were nullified when Shaun crashed through the window.

"What the fuck do you mean you didn't do anything?!" Ethan's voice rings out. "He is my family!"

I start to swing my leg over to get off and demand to know what the fuck the Alpha did to my mate when I feel tiny arms wrap around my middle.

Fuck...

Jack is my responsibility.

Determined that I will be coming back to demand answers, I start the bike and head for the school. Ric had better not have hurt my mate. Alpha or not, my wolf will fucking destroy him.

26

JOSH

My phone lights up yet again showing Ethan is trying to call me. I've already blocked him in the mind speak after I got a hint of what he wants to talk about. I want to turn off my phone, but then there's a chance that I'll miss Max's call. He calls every morning. If I don't answer, he'll know something is wrong and then I'll have to explain and...

Ethan:
If you don't pick up the f-ing phone I will show up there.

Me:
You don't know where I live

Ethan:
I'll ask Gramps

Me:
he doesn't know

Ethan:
I'll ask Gramps for your Mama's number

You wouldn't DARE! I send to him, unblocking him from the mind speak. I can't afford to have my mother brought into this. She would want to come out here and there's no way I could hide this from her, not in person. She can't know how fucked up I am in the head.

Talk to me, Sully. I didn't even know you and Ric had an altercation. I had to find out from Max that my mate is the reason you've been staying away. Why didn't you come to me? Do you not want to be around me anymore? Were you only nice to me because you have to be?

I hurry to cut him off before he spirals worse than I usually do.

Seems self-blame is a family trait, I send over to him in an attempt to lighten the mood. *It's got nothing to do with you or your mate, even though he needs to work on his poker face now that us vamps are going to be around more often.*

That gets a bit of a chuckle out of him and I crack a bit of a smile myself. Ric really looks like he's smelling swamp gas when a vamp is around, but he's improved to not actively sneering so that's something.

So what happened? Why doesn't anyone know the real reason you've ghosted us? Even your mate thinks it's because of Ric, which isn't good considering Max needs to follow and trust his Alpha.

I sigh and debate with myself whether I should come clean. Even Chase doesn't know the reason I came back. Blaming Ric was the easiest solution, but it was cowardly at best. I guess if anyone is going to understand, it would be Ethan. The only other person who could possibly fathom my reasons would be Celeste, but she had her own issues in the lab.

So you know I'm only like two and a half years older than you, right? I tell him and he sends an affirmation. It's weird when there's no actual words in mind speak, but sometimes feelings and gestures come through just fine.

Well, it was about a year after you were taken to the lab that I went looking for you, not even knowing it was actually you I was looking for. Your friend Shaun was trying to find help. I was running away from my responsibilities, so I decided to help this random young werewolf find his friend.

I was a cocky sixteen-year-old, having just come into my abilities. The advanced healing had only just started to kick in, but I was loving the speed and strength that came with feeding. I was so used to having the stable supply of blood from Uncle Edward's menagerie and cold storage that I didn't understand how weak I would become without it.

It was only a few days later when they caught me. At first, they supplied me only with enough blood so that I could regenerate after they cut me open. They wanted to determine how my body processed the blood versus how humans process food. When they couldn't figure it out, they started to withold the blood to see if I would suffer similar effects to starvation. I healed slower, but it wasn't as bad as it could have been.

At that time, they put me in a room with a skylight. To a normal teenage vampire, the sun would be nearly fatal, especially being starved of blood and needing to heal regularly. I am lucky that my mother's bloodline carries the ability to feed off natural light from the sun and the moon. I'll still get sunburn if I'm outside all day, but only to the extent that a human would. That ability saved my life and made it so I wouldn't starve to death.

I could feel the fear, sadness, and anger through the connection with my cousin. We didn't meet inside until I was in there for almost a year. He didn't know me through the time I cried for my Mama every day. He knows what those people were like. He knows the screams, the pain, the hunger, the thirst...

Once the battle royale started, they moved me from the skylight room and started to give me blood again. At first, I didn't think anything of it. It took almost two years for me to realize where the blood was coming from. They were draining the losers, killing them, and feeding them to me.

As soon as I made the connection, I stopped drinking. I refused to bring my fangs out. Then, they found a way to force the issue...

I haven't shared this with anyone, not even Chase. He wouldn't understand. Ethan knows. He understands the fear of making a connection with someone only to have to wonder if today is the day you'll have to watch them die. I can do this. I can tell him. He will understand.

After Erica, the she-wolf from that Michigan pack, lost they took me into a room with a big metal coffin looking thing. They forced me to lay in there and chained me down. I didn't think anything of it at first because it wasn't the first time they put me in something like this. I mean, they drowned me in a similar way multiple times. You remember the drowning tub, right?

But they drowned me when I was sleeping in the sun room. I didn't realize how weak I had become from not having anything to feed on.

After they had me chained up, they brought in Erica.

She was still alive, Ethan...

I curl up into a ball in the corner of my kitchen floor and start to sob. I don't want to remember anymore. I never want to remember this. I was still a kid. I mean legally, I was an adult but they stole my innocence in that moment.

Erica had a little brother and sister she wanted to get home to. She told us all about them and their antics and how the only reason she wasn't home was because her mate wasn't in her home pack.

I get it, Ethan sends to me in a soft tone. *They destroyed us in there and now we're still trying to find the pieces worth putting back together.*

I hug my knees tighter and let out a strangled laugh. It is the farthest thing from funny, but just really fucked up how accurate that is.

I sometimes wonder if it's even worth it to put me back together, I send back. To other people, this thought would send them racing to me, to comfort me or placate me. They'd hurry to reassure me that I'm worth it, special, blah blah, blah. That they need me here or the world wouldn't be the same without me. It's all empty words from someone who hasn't lived in hell. I can't say through hell because parts of us will never make it out of there.

But Ethan doesn't respond like that. He understands. He knows because he was there. He feels exactly what I do. We're broken and always will be broken. There is no cure. There is no magic fix for what was done to us.

Is Erica a piece to pick up or does she get hidden away? Ethan sends to me when he feels I've calmed down a bit. *Do we try to patch this up or pretend it never happened?*

As much as I want to shove all of that time into the back of my mind and pretend it never happened, I know that I need to face it. I at least need to face this one thing. I owe it to her for what I've done.

I need to take a trip, I tell him, hoping that my sanity holds out long enough to possibly bring some peace to someone who might be able to reach it. I'm pretty sure we are both lost causes at this point.

27

MAX

Pulling back up to the house after dropping Jack off at school, I am surprised to see Ric and Ethan standing in the driveway. Well, at least this saves me the steps to tell off my Alpha.

"Before you flip out, you need to listen," Ric says, holding up his hand as I dismount from my bike. "Ethan has talked to his cousin and things are a bit clearer now."

Tucking my helmet under my arm, I turn my attention to the smaller man in front of me. Ethan looks more diminished than I can remember seeing him in a very long time. Whatever he and Josh discussed has shaken him and pulled him a little bit back into that place he was before. I offer him a small smile of encouragement, but the pain in his eyes doesn't go away.

In fact, Ethan turns and runs inside. I look at my friend in question, but he just shakes his head with a frown. "Not my story to tell even if I knew the details," he tells me. "They used their mind speak thingy and whatever was shared..."

My Alpha takes a deep breath before continuing. I can see the shadows in his expression, so I have a pretty good idea at this point as to the content of the discussion.

"Let's just say, we are *all* in this together, brother. I'm here for the both of you, whenever or whatever you need," he tells me, pulling me into a one-armed hug.

The anger I felt towards my Alpha when I pulled up isn't there anymore, but instead I feel rage toward myself. My mate has been struggling for weeks, avoiding everyone who loves him, and I did not even know. I'm such a piece of shit.

"I need to go see him," I tell Ric as soon as he releases me. "I can't believe I didn't notice..."

"Don't blame yourself," he interrupts. "I misread a lot with Ethan, as you are already aware. It's easy to overlook it when they actively work to hide their pain. You know that better than almost anyone else. If I didn't have the archived school reports or been witness to your extremely rare drunken outbursts, I wouldn't know even a quarter of your past and what you've been through."

I hang my head in shame at that last part. That is exactly the reason I hate myself for missing the signs with Josh. I've been abused. I know what it's like to pull away to keep someone from seeing. When I lift my head to look at my Alpha again, he is giving me a knowing look.

"It was easier to let you think the problem was me," he tells me. "I was hoping he would turn to you, and it would all come out naturally, but I underestimated the Sullivan stubbornness."

That gets a small chuckle out of me. When we were kids, we all saw the stubborn streak that ran within Ethan and often wondered where he got it because Connor *didn't* have it. Actually, looking back, it makes a ton more sense now knowing that they aren't biologically brothers. Apparently, the stubborn thing comes from Ethan's mother's father's side of the family.

"The Heartstones aren't any better," Ethan's voice drifts out from the open doorway, and I raise my eyebrow glancing at Ric. "If you're done talking about me, can you give him his mission already so that I can go play before the babies wake up again?"

Mission?

Ric laughs, and the light seems to come back to his expression again. Whatever heaviness was discussed between the cousins, it doesn't seem to be hopeless.

"I'm sending you to check out my grandfather's pack," he tells me before pinching his chin. "Well, technically now I believe it is my uncle's pack. I don't even know if my grandfather is still alive."

He seems deep in thought for a few moments before he shakes himself out of it and continues, "Either way, it's my mother's side of the family. I never met any of them except my Uncle Aaron, but as you are well aware, he died when my parents did. They never even showed for the funeral, so I ignored them in return.

"*But*, Ethan wants the triplets to know where they come from, even if it's only just knowing who is still alive. So, I need you to go up there, find out who remains of the Snowden family, and ascertain if they are the kind of people you would trust with Jack and the babies."

Considering how Ethan only found out who his birth parents were less than a year ago, I can't say I blame him for wanting to know everything for his kids' sake. What I don't understand, however, is why I have to be the one to go on this recon mission. This could easily be accomplished by any one of the warriors under me, especially those who are single under the guise of looking for their mate.

"Why me?" I ask and proceed to give voice to my concerns. I am responsible for the security of the entire pack as head warrior. Additionally, there are more vulnerable members in the pack than ever before, and our Beta is still being a little fuckwit because of his feelings of inadequacy. It's not the right time for the head warrior to be away from the pack...

"It's also for your mate," Ric tells me in a whisper. "The only thing Ethan would tell me after his conversation with his cousin was that Josh needs to visit the pack in Michigan to make something right. Your mate is convinced he needs to go there, and no one will protect him better than you. I don't want my boy to lose anyone else. He's lost enough in this lifetime."

If my choice is between protecting the pack and protecting my mate, there is no choice. Fuck the pack.

"I'll need a car to use," I call back to him as I rush toward my room to pack. "You still haven't replaced the hunk of scrap we hauled off the front lawn last week."

"There's a hybrid something or other in the garage," he says with a laugh, and I put the last of the clothes I might need in my suitcase. Glancing at the closet, I see the bag of remaining goodies on the topmost shelf. It's the last of my Christmas present from Ethan...

Could I possibly need grenades on this trip?

28

JOSH

Ethan:
Pack up. Maxi-pad is taking you to Michigan.

Me:
WTF dude! Secret much?

Ethan:
Didn't tell. Ric's mom's family is there.

I fibbed a bit.

Said I want to know if the trips should get to know them

It gives you an excuse to be in the pack so you can check on Erica's family. You don't have to even say anything about her if you're not ready, but at least this way you can see that they're alright.

Okay, so my cousin is a smartass, but smart seems to be the operative word. I can't deny that his plan is pretty airtight. I mean, having the head warrior visit the relatives to do a danger assessment after the Alpha's kid is born used to be a standard practice. I mean, it's basically null and void these days since Uncle Edward would slaughter any Alpha who would even consider killing babies. But it was common enough in the history books that most packs will still accept those visits.

So they'll let Max in, but I'm a vampire. Newsflash, Cuz. Most other supes only tolerate us because Uncle Edward can wipe them out. They'd never welcome me in, especially without an entourage. And even if they do, I'll never be allowed near anyone but the warriors.

I don't bother packing anything yet because at best, Max will have to scout everything out *for* me. That means I have to tell him what happened. I'm not ready to tell him. I like the fact that he doesn't look at me like I'm fragile, like I'm ten seconds away from shattering. If I tell him, I will lose him... or at least the version of him that I love.

Wait... love?

I love him. Holy fucking shitknockers! I love Max.

They can't deny him from bringing his mate, Ethan says in my head. I'm still reeling from my personal revelation so I don't quite catch his meaning until he adds: *You just have to mark each other and they'll never deny it.*

Mark him? That means I'd have to bite him, draw blood.

I can't mark him! I send back to Ethan in a panic. *No blood. I can't do blood. I told you this already! This won't work...*

I start pulling at my hair in my fear and frustration before pulling the few things I started to pack out of my bag. How in the hell can I risk it? Chase has almost died more than a few times thanks to the blood issue. The only reason he survived was because he's willing to temporarily hurt me to subdue my fight response in my panic attacks. Max will never hurt me. I'll end up killing my mate!

Well, you have a twelve plus hour drive to figure it out, Ethan sends me right before I hear the beep of a horn outside of my building. *Trust in the bond between fated mates. Fate gave you one of the best men I've ever met. You can let go with him.*

As I wipe the tears from my eyes, there is a knock at my door. I rush through packing my bag using my vampire speed, hoping I don't forget anything vital like deodorant or clean underwear, before I open the door for Max. He searches my face and I know he can see the evidence of my morning freak out. But instead of asking about it, he just takes my bag from me and heads toward the stairs.

I guess it's time for a long and awkward road trip.

29

MAX

I don't question him about the fact that he was obviously crying this morning. I don't even ask him how his day is going. Instead, I have spent the last eight and a half hours listening to an audio book that started as a game of never have I ever and ended up with roommates getting together. When the book ends, I am beyond ready to talk to him. This silent treatment isn't going to work if we're going to be facing another pack tomorrow.

"Book two is even better," he tells me before I can say anything. "It's a whole thing with a misunderstanding and there's an app and the one guy is actually a stripper and..."

I snatch the phone from his hands and place it between my legs. Not that the book doesn't sound interesting, but I know he is using it to hide from me. It hurts to know he doesn't trust me enough to tell me what is wrong.

"We are about to stop for the night," I announce to cut off his protest before it can start. "I don't want to surprise the Alpha up there by showing up this late in the day with no warning. Nor do I want to show up stinky and tired from driving all day. We have roughly a four hour drive ahead of us tomorrow, so let's save the next book for that."

In my peripheral vision, I see Josh swallow nervously and sit on his hands before he nods. If there is one thing that therapy got through my head after Ms. Anna dragged me in for it, it's that you can't force someone to talk before they are ready to. As much as my wolf and inner alpha bristle at not being able to command it, I know I just have to wait for my mate to be ready to talk to me.

Using the GPS built into the car, I locate the closest mid range hotel for us to stay the night. Even though I know the sunlight doesn't appear to be problematic for my mate, I don't want to take any chances with someone being able to open a door and have the outside pouring into the room while he is asleep and vulnerable.

"What? No Four Seasons?" Josh asks with a smirk when we pull into the parking lot. "You wolves have no sense of class."

It takes my caveman, *please my mate*, centric brain to recognize that he's joking. During one of his rare trips to the house before the babies were born, I happened to eavesdrop on a conversation between him and Ethan in the playroom. I think they were having a tea party or something with the stuffies at the time.

"More tea, good sir?" Ethan asked in a horridly fake British accent.

"Oh but this tea is too pedestrian, poor chap," Josh replied with a more natural accent. "You need to have dried it for ten days in the rays of the last sunset of summer overlooking a baboon's red arse in the jungle for it to be worthy of a prince of the vampires."

Both boys descended into chaotic giggles while I went off in search of the Alpha to report in.

That day was the first time I realized that the pretentious attitude that Edward put forth was not the way Josh saw himself or even expected to be treated. It was one of the first times I truly thanked fate for giving me the man that they did. As one of the poorest members of my pack, I was really worried about the materialistic disparity between us. Knowing that Josh didn't care at all about money or expensive things was a relief I didn't even know I needed at the time.

"Perhaps this poor chap can only manage something so pedestrian," I tell him in my own laughable attempt at a cockney accent. Glancing at his face, I bark out a rough laugh. He is just so fucking confused and it's hilarious. I'm still laughing as I grab our bags from the trunk and head for the lobby. He rushes to catch up to me, hooking his arm through mine.

"Did you listen in on the tea party somehow?" he asks. I'm glad to see the light is coming back in his eyes. He giggles when I nod, so I give him a quick peck to the side of his head. I love the fact that although he is not exactly short by human standards, he is so much smaller than I am. As an alpha wolf, being six foot five inches is about average, maybe an inch one way or the other. At five foot ten inches, Josh would be considered tall if compared to almost any other race.

The hotel clerk asks us the usual questions at the desk, but Josh isn't paying attention and staring at the floor. I might have felt some concern about his stillness if he wasn't smiling and hugging my arm like it's his favorite stuffie.

"East or west facing windows?" the clerk asks, tearing my attention away from my mate.

"West," I say at the same time Josh says, "East."

I look at him and he shrugs before answering, "I like to watch the sun come up," he says nonchalantly. "It's why I don't mind so much being on the east coast. Sometimes, I often wonder if the sunrise looks different in different parts of the country. I've seen it from Maine to Florida along the coast. Louisiana was interesting. My uncle let me ride on one of barges when I was like ten to go out and watch it from the middle of the Mississippi when Mama wasn't paying attention. I'm trying to work my way through all fifty states and have managed in every one I've been in except Ohio. I never got to see the sun come up in Ohio back when..."

His voice trails off as I watch his expression fall. I know exactly what he's thinking about and I want to get him up to the room quickly. He doesn't need the clerk and other people in the lobby to see his pain.

"East facing," I tell the clerk and she hands over two key cards with polite but concerned smile. The envelope says 216 and she points to the sign for the elevators for me. I appreciate that she is able to read the situation and not bring more attention to us. She has my card number and the room number if she needs anything else, but I doubt she will use it. This might be the first time ever I use one of those stupid surveys to praise an employee, because this clerk is a saint.

When the elevator doors close, I lift Josh into my arms. Right now, I need to get my boy into our room. This is the biggest reason I wanted to stop for the night. My mate isn't exactly mentally ready for whatever he needs to face in Michigan. I only wish I knew what it was so that I could be prepared as well.

30

JOSH

Mentally, I checked out from the time it finally registered to my brain that I am back in Ohio. The only reason I stayed silent and somewhat sane was the fact that Max had a tight grip on my arm. As soon as he picked me up in the elevator, I let my mind go and clung to him like he was a life preserver and I was drowning surrounded by sharks.

Oh, fuck me running, I do *not* need to be thinking about sharks right now.

When the door to our room closes with us on the inside, I lose my internal battle and start giggling like a lunatic. I'm giggle-snorting and crying and a million kinds of mess but refuse to let go of my mate. Instead of forcing me to get down, Max just proceeds to set our bags down on the dresser in the room. He then pulls out fresh clothes for each of us and our toiletries to prepare for the night. The fact that he's acting like this is all normal only makes it seem that much more absurd, and I laugh even harder.

After what must have been at least ten minutes, I think I am finally calming down. Max pats me on the bottom and asks, "You get it all out, Little One?"

I give a weak giggle and nod before I unclench my hands to slide down the front of his body. The feel of such a hard body is a pleasure I don't often allow myself to indulge in. Too many men have wanted me for what I could do for them or to them. Being the heir has been hell on my sex life since I can't really trust that the vampires I meet want to fuck me just to let me get off. They all want *relationships*... more like they want a status boost.

"Don't start something you aren't willing to follow through with, boy," Max growls and grips my hips, pulling me flush against his front. I can feel a certain part of him growing hard against the front of my body and I fucking *yearn* to take that dick inside of me. I never understood the difference between merely wanting and *yearning* until this fucking moment.

"I'll follow that dick anywhere," I mutter and then slap my hand over my mouth in shock.

That was supposed to be an inside thought...

Max chuckles and moves his hands to my ass cheeks to give them a squeeze. "You sure you don't want to be in front? If you want, it can be right at home, right here."

My eyes roll as I moan in response. The sound is muffled by my hands that are still covering my mouth, but Max has no issue catching my drift when he lifts me up by gripping my ass. Wrapping my legs around his waist again, I bury my face in his neck to hide my embarrassment as he carries us into the bathroom.

31

JOSH

The sound of the shower turning on makes me lean back to look at what kind of facilities we are working with. The bathroom in this place is more spacious than the one at my apartment, which is surprising considering Chase paid out of pocket to double the size of ours so that his giant ass could wash his hair without having to do yoga in the shower. This bathroom would easily accommodate someone of his size, plus a few others.

That's actually a very good thing considering my mate is about the same size as my roommate and the only gymnastics I want him doing in the shower is whatever is necessary to *do* me.

"Clean first, Baby," Max says as he slides me down his front again, slower and more deliberate than before. "If you're good, you'll get a treat."

The corners of my lips turn up at that thought. *I like treats.* He gives me a light tap on my ass before pulling my shirt over my head. I hear the quick intake of his breath while my t-shirt is still covering my face, and I close my eyes. I don't want to see if it was a good gasp or a horrified gasp. Out of those of us that made it out of hell alive, only Ethan doesn't carry any physical reminders on his skin. Celeste hides her scars with a glamour. I don't have that luxury.

I feel Max's finger run across my cheek and I flinch, not expecting it.

"Easy, Josh," he murmurs. "Don't cry, baby. If this is too much, we don't have to do anything. I won't hurt you like they did."

Huh?

His words make me open my eyes to look at him. I'm not surprised that I was crying. I'm wondering how in the hell he thinks I wouldn't want him to ravish and love me. I give him the look his words deserve and know I have no choice but to say something.

"You would never hurt me," I tell him honestly. "I just... Well, I'm afraid you would think less of me, not want me, after seeing the scars. To be honest, I forget they're even there anymore. The ones from the last day, those ones were fresh wounds when I was found, so magic was able to heal those without scarring. *Those* would have been some horrific scars.

"But these?" I say indicating my chest and stomach, "These are reminders that I refused them. They remind me that I didn't play their game. I fought as much as I could. They remind me that *I* got out of there... even when so many others didn't make it."

He puts the lid down on the toilet so that he can take a seat and pulls me into the space between his legs. If I were a human, I would worry about the force of his hug cracking a rib or two, but I can handle it. I actually love it. The only thing I couldn't handle right now is if he were to treat me like something breakable. I have had enough of people walking on eggshells around me.

"I don't know how others have reacted to your scars," Max says, still hiding his face from me. "But to me, they are perfection. Scars show what we have survived, and you are so incredibly strong to have survived so much. You are so much more than I could ever deserve, but I'm going to be selfish for once in my damn life and keep you... even though I'm not worthy."

His words touch something deep inside of me, and I reach down his back to rip his shirt off. I need to get to his bare skin. Fuck his thoughts of being unworthy. Fuck my thoughts of being broken. It's high time I just trust fate and get to the fucking.

32

MAX

The sound of my shirt getting shredded by my mate's claws seems to flip the switch in me from "Cuddle" to "Let's Make Some Porn" pretty fucking quickly. I reach for the button on his jeans and flick them open. I hope I don't damage the zipper when I yank them down to his knees, but I'm in too much of a hurry right now. I can buy him new pants if I need to.

Great googly moogly...

Thoughts of pants shopping vacate my brain as I notice Josh isn't wearing underwear. I had been sitting in an enclosed space with my mate going commando for the last nine fucking hours, and I'm only just now finding out. It's a good thing I didn't know before now or I might have wrecked the Alpha's brand-new car.

I can't seem to stop staring at Josh's erect penis in front of me. There are overlapping latticework of scars all *around* his genitals, but it is almost as if his tormenters couldn't bring themselves to harm that part of him. The lack of scars makes it seem even more significant, more precious. For the first time in my life, I feel the urge to put my mouth on a dick. I want to feel it, taste it...

No, it's only him. I want to feel Josh, taste Josh. So, I do.

Wrapping my hand around the base of his dick, I realize my hand is able to cover well over half of his length. If I had to wager a guess, I would say he is around average at five, maybe six inches in length. But the sight of him disappearing into my fist as I start to stroke up and down gives me a possessive thrill. I *like* that I am so much bigger than him. That has never happened before.

In the past, I tended to avoid being with men so much smaller than me in stature. I refused to be with anyone who I feared couldn't overpower me if necessary. Not many can, so the number of partners I've had is relatively low. The worry I used to carry just isn't present with Josh. As a vampire, I know he can throw me through the damn wall if he wanted to, so I don't have to hold back my strength or urges with him. For the first time in my life, I am free to just feel my own feelings and enjoy what I enjoy.

I give my wrist a little twist at the end of my stroke up Josh's dick and he makes a startled squeaking noise that I want to hear more of. I've never heard that kind of noise from a partner before. I want to spend the rest of our lives figuring out what other noises I can make come out of him.

Leaning forward, I lick the precum from his tip as I move my fist back toward his body. I open the last three fingers on my hand so only my forefinger and thumb are gripping him as I lick him from base to tip in one swipe, loving the salty musk taste I get from his skin. I really love that his scent reminds me of popcorn and trips to the movies. Maybe when we're back home, we can play around with some melted butter.

The squawk that comes out of Josh's mouth when I take him into my mouth and apply some suction sounds like it should belong to one of those exotic birds rich people seem to collect, not a twenty four year old man. I let out a chuckle around him. I am not prepared when his knees give out in response.

Pulling my hand away from the base of his dick, I release him from my mouth so that I can catch him with both of my hands. But when my palms make contact with his ass, it is apparently enough to send him over the edge. His release paints my face, hair and chest, along with a good portion of the bathroom, as I struggle to hold him upright while keeping my eyes closed to prevent his cum from actually blinding me. I love how reactive my mate is in his orgasm, even with the additional mess created by his spasms.

When his orgasm finally subsides, I make sure he's leaning his weight on me so that I can finish getting him undressed for the shower. I feel down his legs to fully remove his pants, socks, and shoes. As soon as I am sure he is naked, I stand up myself, holding his noodle like body against my chest so that I can remove my own pants, making sure to keep my eyes shut. Cum in the eyes is not fun, or so I've heard.

Once I am as sure as I can be without opening my eyes that we are both completely devoid of our clothing, I use my free hand to feel along the wall, to guide me on our way into the shower. As soon as I feel the water, I put my face under the spray to rinse away his release. I'm glad I didn't skimp on the hotel for this shower alone.

"That was amazeballs," Josh mumbles into my chest as he wraps his arms around my middle. He sounds half drunk and I can't help the smile creeping across my face.

Mate is satisfied. Good job, man-form, my wolf says to me in a smug tone. I laugh out loud at the absurdity of it. I have never heard of a wolf caring about the sexual activities of their human half. Well, as long as they weren't unfaithful to their mate, that is. But apparently my wolf has to put his two cents in. Then again, my wolf has always seemed to have a bit more humanity than others.

"Did your wolf just congratulate you?" Josh asks as he turns his back to my front to get the water to rinse away the cum from his own body. "Or was I imagining that?"

I laugh again and grab my body wash from the shelf where I put it earlier. Lathering up a washcloth, I start to wipe down my mate's body before I answer him. "You didn't imagine it," I tell him. "My wolf has a special interest in making you satisfied and happy and safe. You are the only mate he will ever have after all."

Josh turns his back to the water and looks up at me. "Just him?" he asks. His tone is mocking, but there is a vulnerability in his eyes.

"You're it for me, for both of us," I tell him honestly. "From the moment you ran away on that beach, he knew you were it for us. My stupid human brain took longer to give up on the guilt to let me deserve you, but even then I knew there was no one better in this world than you."

Instead of responding, he grabs his body was and pours some onto another washcloth. Throwing my head back, I try to keep calm. I fucked this all up, didn't I? He's going to wash himself, wash away the scent of me and …

I flinch at the feeling of a washcloth moving along the ridges of my abs, working up my chest. He's washing me, marking me in his own scent. My wolf rumbles a sound of appreciation.

Is that a fucking purr? Since when do wolves purr?

"I still worry sometimes," Josh says as he moves the cloth across my collarbone and down each of my arms. "I know how you felt about Ethan. You truly loved him and I can't even fault you for that. He is amazing."

33

JOSH

I push Max's shoulder to get him to turn around so I can wash his back. This is a conversation that needed to happen a long time ago, but life kept getting in the way. My mate was in love with my cousin – my miraculous, gifted, blessed by the fates, prophesied cousin. I'm just the extra vampire princeling who was dumb enough to get captured.

When I don't say anything more, Max reaches behind him and pulls me to his front to face him. He's blocking the water now, so I shiver a bit at the temperature shift, not at the sight of his glorious piece of manflesh pointing at me like it's daring me to give it a go. Yep, it's the temperature.

"First of all," he says, lifting my head with his fingers under my chin. "Both you and your cousin need to stop bastardizing classic literature before I can't read my favorite books ever again."

Oops. I guess that was another inside thought leaking out.

"Secondly," he continues as he moves his palm to cup my cheek, "Your cousin is my best friend, my chosen brother. I will always love him, but in the same way that you do. He is family to me. Honestly, he is the only family I will likely ever claim until you allow me into yours."

I just stare at him in confusion as he leans down to kiss me gently on the lips. This time, there is no heat, no struggling to catch a rhythm or fight for oxygen. This is comfort. This is...

"Do you love me?" I ask before I can think better of it. My eyes widen, and I back away quickly.

"Don't worry about it. Forget I asked," I say hurriedly as I jump out of the shower and grab a towel to wrap around my waist. "I'll just... I'm gonna go out and get ready for bed, let you finish up in here.... Um yeah."

I race from the room using vamp speed for the whopping fifteen feet it takes to get back to the dresser where our bags are. I don't know if it's wishful thinking, but I can almost swear I hear him whisper, "Yes, I love you, Joshua Sullivan," as the door to the steam filled room closes.

What am I doing?

I just got a mind-scrambling orgasm from my mate, and I am running away like a virgin at a demonic sacrifice convention. What the fuck is wrong with me? I don't run from sex! I can take it... and ooooh LAWD do I wanna take Max. I need advice, but who the fuck can I talk to about this?

I start digging through my bag, looking for my phone to call Ethan, or maybe Chase? Fuck, I need more friends. I pull almost everything out, and I can't find the damn thing. I know I brought it because we were using it in the car for the audio book... the car. Did Max leave my phone in the car?

I quickly throw on a pair of shorts from where they landed on the chair and grab the keys to the car along with a room card so I can go down and look. But before I can even grab the door handle, my uncle breaks into my mind. I let out a sigh and thank the heavens that this didn't happen five minutes ago. I definitely do *not* need the memory of my first orgasm with my mate tainted by coitus interruptus of the parental unit variety.

Joshua, where are you? Chase says you are not at home, and I need you, as my heir, to represent me for an urgent issue.

I roll my eyes and throw the keys and room card back on the little desk. I am no longer in a hurry to get to my phone now. Any good or sexy mood I might have been in was effectively killed with his command, but at least now I get to have the pleasure of telling my king to fuck off. And he actually won't be able to get mad at me this time, not unless he wants to upset his newly re-discovered grandson who gave him great-grandbabies.

Sorry, Uncle Edward, I send to him as I launch myself backwards onto the bed in full on starfish position. *I'm already on a mission for Ethan. I mean, I can come back if you insist, but he said I'm the only one he can trust with this.*

I know I'm being immature and petty, but I don't give a shit at this point. I'm tired of his treatment of me bouncing between like I'm an imbecile or I'm supposed to be a trained monkey dancing upon command. This kind of turnabout is exhilarating for me.

Even so, I need to at least try to maintain my composure. If I let even the slightest bit of joy or mirth through, he will know, and I'll have to deal with an even bigger stick up his ass when I get back. He, however, does not hide his feelings from me in the connection. I feel his surprise, his annoyance, followed by his pride, and his resignation all before he deigns to give me a reply. There is a brief flash of hope that the flicker of pride is for me standing up to him before his next words squash it.

If my grandson sent you somewhere, complete his task first. I will have to delay the meeting with the Michigan wolves until either his business is complete or I am available.

WAIT! I send out before he cuts off the connection. It would be a bitch to have him show up in the middle of everything. I can't have him finding out about Erica and why I am really at that pack. *Ethan sent Max and I to Michigan, to meet with the Snowden Pack. We will be arriving there around noon. What is the task you need done? I should be able to take care of it while we're there.*

I'm slightly distracted by the soft groan coming from the bathroom, so I don't really listen to what my uncle is saying until the water shuts off.

... and they want answers about their child. I've sent you the details in an email. Please, do check your phone more often and keep Chase informed. He cannot do his job properly if he does not know where you are.

I acknowledge the reprimand without feeling any real remorse and the connection is terminated. Uncle Edward doesn't really care about my safety. He just doesn't want to suffer the embarrassment of losing another heir.

Before my brain takes me down the self-pity spiral that usually comes with dismissal from my regent, Max comes out of the bathroom wearing nothing but a towel and pity takes a backseat for a brief moment. My dick gives a half-hearted hurrah before giving up under the weight of the conversation I was forced to have.

"Were you going to go somewhere?" my mate asks as he pulls on a pair of gray sweat pants from the clothing he set out on the dresser. Of fucking course, he packed gray sweats. Ugh I'm going to swallow my tongue before the sun even sets.

34

MAX

I was worried that I pushed Josh too far in the shower when I heard him grab the car keys and move toward the door. Whatever stopped him, I am grateful that he stayed. I was fully prepared to beg for forgiveness when I came out of the bathroom. But judging by the look on his face right now, I think he wants more of the same treatment, possibly going up a level or two in the difficulty.

Ugh, I've been spending way too much time with Ethan, Shaun, and Zach during their gaming sessions. Shaun brought his PS-5 over the house while he was staying during the end of Ethan's pregnancy. They made me jump in to play when Seb wasn't available as the fourth player. None of them liked it when someone would have to sit out because of an odd number. With Ethan in little mode and Zach being an obvious middle, Shaun often looked to me to help him wrangle the other boys. I'm terrible at video games, but they insisted that me playing was more than fair because Ethan falls into his little space, all he manages to do is button mash. Now, I'm talking about sex as if it's a multi-level video game.

"Ummm," Josh says before whipping his head back quickly. "I was just gonna check and see if my phone was in the car. I couldn't find it in my bag."

I pick the towel up from where I set it on the chair to start drying my hair a bit. I point toward the dresser where I laid out our clothes for the next morning. "I set both our phones over there with our clothes. There are spots on the top for wireless charging, so I figured they could charge up a bit while we were in the shower."

He looks a bit embarrassed that he didn't check there. I chuckle as he drags his feet like a scolded child to go over and grab his phone. Josh frowns when the screen lights up. It becomes a full body cringe when he unlocks the device. He presses a few things and winces. This seems to repeat over and over at least a dozen times, and I have to ask.

"Bad news?" I throw the towel back into the bathroom on the floor. If we were planning on staying more than just the night, I would hang it up. I'm not an animal... at least not in how I treat people.

"Not bad per say," Josh shrugs before looking away from the screen to meet my eyes. "Just over a dozen messages from Chase trying to find out where I am so that he could try to run interference with my uncle. He knows I'm with you, but that's all I told him. When he informed Uncle Edward that he didn't know where I was, I got brain blasted by the liege lord.

"He wants me to go as his representative for something and, as usual, assumed I had nothing better to do with my time. But, this task he has for me is with the very same pack we are going to be visiting, so now I have an official reason to be there and they can't kick me out for being a random vampire in their territory. I'm just waiting on the email with the details."

Right after he finishes talking, his screen lights up. I walk over to him and pull him back against me, reading over his shoulder. Blah... Blah... Blah... a bunch of bureaucratic bullshit reminding Josh of his place and responsibilities as the heir to the vampire king...

The family you are to meet with is the Neeley family. Their daughter's remains were returned to them almost a year ago. They had a forensic witch do a magical autopsy for cause of death and it was determined to be exsanguination. They want recompense from the ones responsible and you are there to ensure we have enough information to punish the vampire who drained their daughter.

My wolf goes on alert inside of me. Something is very wrong, but

I can't hear or smell anyone approaching the room. I'm ashamed to admit it takes me way too long to realize my mate is frozen in my arms. He's even stopped his heartbeat.

35

JOSH

They are going to kill me.

A month ago, fuck that, even a week ago, I would have welcomed it. I know I deserve it. But now, I have Max. I have someone who wants me, *the real me,* even with the scars. I only just found a little slice of happiness. Why the fuck do I have to lose it?

"Baby? What's the matter?" Max asks as he takes the phone from my hands to set it back down on the dresser. "Let's lay down and talk it out. I'm not leaving you, no matter what it is."

Oh gods, he's going to die too! He'll never let them kill me. I'm his mate. Wolves are so much more protective of their mates, even to a fault. They'll have to kill him to get to me. Is it too late to send him home?

"You should leave me," I whisper when he pulls me onto his chest in the bed. He has to be the one to leave. I don't have the strength to leave him. I don't fucking care if I'm a coward anymore. I can't run from him again, not even for his own good.

He growls at my words and holds me tighter, as if I would try to escape. "I'm never leaving you," he tells me. "And if you know what's good for you, you'll never leave me again."

I bury my face in his chest and tell him the truth, "I'm not brave enough to leave you again."

Such. A. Fucking. Coward.

Max's hold on me softens and I panic, grabbing onto him, refusing to let go. "Please don't let me go. Don't hate me, please! I can be better! I'll do better!"

He moves his hands to my back and starts to run them over me in circles. It takes a while, but eventually the message gets through my fear that he isn't letting go. He isn't leaving me. He was merely relaxing his hold for comfort.

"No more of this better bullshit," he tells me when my breathing returns to normal. Was I having a panic attack? "The only person who you need to be better for, or to, is yourself, alright Little One?"

I don't really know what he means by that, but I nod anyways. My mate doesn't want an obedient little drone. He's proven that over and over again. I just have to remember that.

"Now, what was it about that email got you so upset?" he asks, and I feel my heart stutter in my chest again. He is going to hate me. He is going to realize how fucked up I am. But he would have found out tomorrow anyways when we reach the Snowden Pack.

"For starters," I begin with a shaky voice, "I don't need to do an investigation to find out what happened to Erica Neeley because I am the vampire that killed her."

I wince at Max's sharp intake of breath. I'm pretty certain it was involuntary on his part, but it still hurts. I guess it's a good thing that he thinks so highly of me that he didn't believe I could kill someone. I mean, I am only twenty-four and spent at least five years locked up, so it's not like I have had a whole lot of free time to screw up like that.

"Was it self-defense?" he asks me. I love this man so much for having faith in me, as unfounded as it is. I shake my head and know he can feel the movement. I can't bear to look up and see the disappointment on his face.

"No, it wasn't self-defense," I tell him. "Her death was very much deliberate and the direct result of my choices."

I open my mind to my mate to show him the memory. Once he sees it, he will understand. If he knows, he'll keep himself safe tomorrow when I have to face her family. He will let me face the consequences of my actions.

36

JOSH

Years Ago – In the Lab

Why the fuck are these dumbasses using steel to hold a vampire? Don't they know you need an enchantment or silver, preferably both, to hold one of us?

While Noah and Pete leave me in this gods awful excuse for a coffin, I flex and shift to try and budge the chains. The one is caught in my leg hair and the pull is rather annoying.

Nothing happens. The chains don't budge. Hell, my body doesn't move under my command. It's like I'm wrapped in cement from the chest down. Everywhere the chains touch seems to be frozen.

Wait – why did nothing happen? This is just regular steel, right? I don't feel any enchantments. There's no silver content in this metal. I would definitely feel it; wouldn't I?

"Looks like getting ahold of that demon paid off," Pete says as they come back in the room dragging something behind them. I can't see what they brought with them because the walls of the damn container are too high. "The itty-bitty vampire can't seem to get out on his own this time."

The two of them laugh as I hear more chains being moved around and a lock snapping closed. I have no clue what is going on. I can't see anything but the ceiling above me and the dull gray of the steel surrounding me. However, I know that if they are laughing, I'm not going to like whatever it is they have brought into the room with them. Summoning as much bravado as I can manage, I try to bluff my way out of this.

"If you're going to suffocate or drown me, can you make it quick? I need to catch up on my beauty sleep."

They laugh.

Fuck, that's never a good sign.

I hear a thump followed by a groan that I vaguely recognize. I figured they brought someone in to make me feed on them, but usually the person is already dead, or at least a stranger – one of the unfortunate victims that are too scared of the fact that I have fangs to talk to me. But I know this voice.

Please, gods, let me be wrong...

I hear metal grating on metal as the pulley machine starts to raise my intended victim into position above me. I know my eyes are reflecting the fear I see in Erica's own emerald eyes. Ignoring the voices of the monsters in the room with us, we stare at each other. We know that at least one of us is likely going to die in this room today if we don't figure out the game plan fast enough.

"Tell my family I did my best to come home to them," she whispers into my mind. She is one of the few who is aware I even have that ability. She taught Ethan a lot about how to fight using his wolf. "You need to survive. You need to make sure they all pay. You have the connections to make it happen."

I thrash my head violently, wishing I could move my body and escape. I won't kill one of my few friends. They can't make me do it. I will refuse. They might kill us both as a result, but I won't do it.

I watch as Erica's body starts to lower toward me. My struggles increase, but whatever demon magic was used is enough to hold my body still. There is a calmness in her gaze that I could never match. She has accepted her fate, but I don't want to kill her!

"They want me to feed, right? I'll just take a little bit and they'll take you back and we can escape together," I send to her. Yeah. That's how we'll do it. We can both survive this. I know we can. I'll play their game and we all live to see tomorrow.

When she's right above me, they do their usual demanding me to feed.

Oh, gods, I'm gonna be sick.

I plunge my fangs into Erica's neck and suck on the wound. The blood tastes soooo good, but I can't do it. I can't feed like this! I'm going to vomit.

Pulling away from her neck, I have to breathe through my mouth to stop my stomach from emptying. I just fed on my friend...

I just violated her...

"You tried to save me," she sends to me as she is looking out into the room with concern. "Remember that."

Before I can ask her what she means by that, Noah comes into view with a silver blade and runs it across Erica's throat. He nearly decapitates her in his exuberance. I gag at the look of joy on his face before the gush of her blood obliterates my vision.

I try to close my mouth, but Pete is there before I can manage it, slamming a dental gag in and cranking it open far enough that the sides of my lips have split. I keep turning my head, trying to escape the flow of my friend's blood, but it keeps pouring out of her, slower and slower.

I hear the crank of the chains again and I pray they are pulling her body away, letting my nightmare end. I give them too much credit... I feel another rush of blood. I won't look. I don't want to know what they are doing to her body to make more blood come out, if it's even blood at this point.

Stop thinking, dumbass! I can't let that image in my head. I can only lay here as I feel the level of cooling liquid rises to cover my ears. I feel the container I'm in shift as it rises under my feet, causing the the blood to rush toward the end with my head. My choices are swallow her blood or drown in it.

I want to drown...

"They were friends, right?" Pete's muffled voice interrupts the cadence of the slow drip hitting my cheek. I'm barely able to keep my face out of the liquid by straining my neck to the extreme.

It's just water. It's not Erica's blood. It's not my dead friend's blood...

It's water from a leaky pipe. It's only a leaky pipe dripping on my face.

"Yeah. So?" I hear Noah's response and it sounds like his feet shuffle toward the side of the room.

Pete chuckles before he says, "Maybe they should have one last sleepover for old time's sake?"

Fuck! No! Please no!

Noah laughs and I hear the clinking of the chains. I start to pray to everything I can think of that I just have a very active imagination. They can't be evil enough to do what I think they are doing. The blood has dried on my face, but I ignore the pain of ripping out my eyelashes to wrench my eyes open.

I clench my jaw to hold in the screams and pleas as I watch. I know those fuckers will only get off on them. I can't do a damn thing except stare into the lifeless emerald eyes of Erica Neeley, big sister, warrior's daughter, and friend, as her body gets closer with every clink of the pulley.

My resolve to stay silent lasts only until her cold and lifeless skin touches mine. The sounds ripping out of me are sounds one should only hear in nightmares, but I can't stop. I choke on her blood since I can't scream and keep my head above it any longer. I barely hear the laughter of the two nightmares made flesh in the room with me.

Squeezing my eyes shut, I focus on trying to stop the screaming. As long as I'm scared, they won't quit. If I don't stop screaming, I actually might drown in her blood.

I should have kept my eyes open. Next thing I know, they've slammed a lid on the coffin. I'm trapped in the dark, buried under the weight of my friend's corpse, drowning in her blood. There is no holding back anymore. I scream until there is no air left to breathe. They finally succeeded this time.

I'm broken.

37

MAX

"I am the reason she's dead," Josh whispers after he brings us out of his memory. "Her blood is the last blood that will ever touch my tongue. I can't even smell blood without falling back into the memory of that day. Even my own blood will set me off. My body remembers trying to fight the chains, so I'm a danger to everyone around when I succumb to the memory."

I'm absolutely horrified at what he has just shared with me. Having briefly interacted with both Noah Chastain and this Pete person before being able to bring them to their deaths, I can honestly say they both got off easy. Had I known they had this kind of evil inside of them, I would have killed them much slower.

Can't change past, my wolf says to me, reminding me that our mate is here in the present. The amount of suffering those fuckers did or did not go through in the end doesn't change what they put our mate through.

Josh lets out a harsh bark of laughter before I can say anything. "Yeah, I'm the fucked up vampire prince who can't even be around blood. What kind of a vampire can't drink blood? The kind that will get everyone killed, that's what kind."

I hold him tighter to me even as he starts to struggle a bit. I can tell he's not trying to get away. He just needs a release of some kind, and a fight would give him that. But I don't want to fight with my mate. When I feel the moisture on my chest, I finally let my own tears fall. Even as painful as this is, I can feel that Josh isn't as tense as he has been since the day I met him. There is a feeling of relief coming off of him, now that he's gotten his big secret off his chest.

"You see now? They want to kill the vampire responsible," he whispers into the darkening room. The sun started to set while we were laying here. "I killed her. It's my fault she died that day. If I hadn't refused them for so long, they wouldn't have resorted to that."

I reach down to pull his face up toward my own. I make sure I have eye contact before I contradict what he is saying. I need to make sure he understands this.

"You are not responsible for other people's actions," I growl out using my authority as an alpha wolf. It shouldn't work since I'm technically third in our pack, but my wolf told me long ago that it is a part of my birthright to use as I see fit. "Those men were evil to the core. If you behaved differently, they would have only found another way to torment you and eventually kill both of you. Don't take their guilt upon yourself just because you are here while she is not."

After a few moments, Josh licks his lips and gives me a small smile. "Has anyone ever told you that you sound like a shrink?" he asks.

I chuckle and move my arm back around his back. "Just passing on the wisdom that was given to me once upon a time in therapy, sweetheart."

At that, Josh pushes himself upright into a sitting position.

"You went to therapy?!"

The shock and outrage on his face makes me flash back to when Ethan had the same reaction. I can't deny that it is rather unorthodox for men to seek out therapy, especially ones in power. Add in the wolf and the fact that I'm an alpha and apparently everyone loses their minds at the thought of me in therapy.

"An extremely smart and caring woman convinced a very stubborn teenage me that talking to someone was a better plan than committing murder," I tell him with a laugh. "Although, considering what happened anyways, I sometimes regret not killing the bastards at the time anyways."

"Was she your angel?" he asks as he lays back down.

I feel the tears start to form like they tend to do when I think about Ms. Anna. "Yeah. It was Ms. Anna, the Alpha Mate... Ric's mom. She saved me so many times, but three of them stand out in my mind as defining moments. They were part of the story I told you earlier. Do you remember it all?"

Josh shrugs and mumbles a bit. It almost sounds like he says, "Tell me again," so I do. Only this time, I'm not telling the story of the unnamed little boy. This is really about me, and I want to make sure my mate knows my story.

"First, she saved me from my abuser who was trying to kidnap me when I was around eleven or twelve. At the time, I thought she was an avenging angel sent to destroy the evil in the pack. In reality, she was just out for a walk to clear her head while her mate was fucking my mother."

I hear the gasp of surprise escape Josh. It's practically unheard of for mates to be able to betray each other in that way. From what we are taught growing up, once the bond is in place and both mates are marked, infidelity would cause extreme pain to the one not acting on it. I tried not to think about how much pain Ms. Anna was in over the years, but there is more than one reason I referred to her mate as Alpha Dick.

"How did she..." he can't even finish the question.

"I have no idea how she managed to hide that kind of pain, but she was honestly the strongest woman – no, the strongest person – that I have ever met and probably ever will meet," I tell him. "Well, except maybe you."

I give him a kiss on the top of his head and he squirms. To change the subject away from himself, Josh asks, "What was the second time?"

I smile at the fact that he's being shy with me. I love that he hasn't put his walls back up with me.

"The second time was my first shift," I tell him. "It is supposed to be the father's responsibility to lead their children, especially the sons, in their first shift. In the event that the father is not available, other family or the Alpha of the pack is supposed to step in. Considering those two were busy together in bed that day, I was abandoned to shift alone."

I can almost feel the questions pouring out of him, but he stays silent. This is probably the first time I've actually felt the difference between us, being wolf and vampire. The first shift is one of the biggest things for a shifter of any type, but unless you have a wolf inside of you, there is no way to know or understand the pain or fear of being without a pack. The wolf is not meant to be a solitary creature.

"Pack is everything to the wolf," I explain. "Without a pack, the wolf can become feral and uncontrollable, eventually dragging their human half into insanity. Having one's parent or Alpha present at the first shift lets the wolf know they are part of the pack, that they are accepted, that they are not alone. To abandon a young wolf on his first shift is the same as saying that he is rejected, homeless, and worthless.

"Ms. Anna saved me and my wolf from that. She arrived before my shift began and stayed long after my wolf took physical form. I have never known who my sperm donor was, so I thought it was appropriate that my wolf manifested looking like Ms. Anna's. I know it was just a coincidence, but I like to imagine it was fate showing me I was accepted by her as part of her family."

Josh squeezes me in a slight hug before murmuring sleepily, "I'm glad she was there for you. But that's only two things. What was the third?" His yawn is big enough to...

No sexy thoughts! We need sleep.

"I'll tell you in the morning, Little One," I say as I pull the blanket up over us. "You're barely awake as it is."

"Please?"

I can't say no when he looks up at me with puppy dog eyes.

"She handed me Jackie and made me promise to protect him, even from Ric if I have to. She gave my life purpose again when I wanted to die... after I failed Ethan."

"We all failed him," Josh whispers into the darkness. "And in the end, he still saved us all."

I can't deny that fact. Ethan could have left us all behind. Hell, he almost did a few times. He could have just told us all to fuck off. Instead, he came back and fought with us, *for us*, and saved us all from the deities who tried to subvert the fates. None of us deserve him, but he's chosen us as his family. And being a part of Ethan's family brought me to my own mate.

"Thank the fates for Ethan," I whisper fervently to the night.

As sleep takes over, I swear I hear a woman's laughter and a soft "You're welcome."

38

JOSH

The house in front of us is gigantic. I thought Ethan's house was big, but this is on a whole other level. Did this use to be a resort or something? The fact that I can see the lake behind it worries me a bit. They won't need to do much to dispose of a body here. I mean, Canada is right across that body of water and I'm sure they could stage a moose accident if they needed to...

"Relax, Little One," Max leans over and kisses me on the cheek. "No one is going to hurt you with me here."

"That's what I'm worried about," I mumble when he gets out of the car on his side. I'm going to be the reason my mate loses his life when he has faced so much just to get to this point. He deserves so much more.

I see someone coming out of the front of the house, so I rush to get out of the car and stand with Max. I don't know if Ric ever called ahead to let them know we were coming, but I have zero doubt that Uncle Edward would have informed them of my visit. Judging by the look on the man's face in front of us, they aren't happy that a vampire was sent, especially one who can stand in the noon sun without repercussions.

"Greetings, Prince Joshua," the man greets us like he's chewing on tinfoil. "Mr. and Mrs. Neeley are waiting in the conference room for you with the remains so that you can begin the investigation. Your *bodyguard* can wait out here."

Max growls and takes a step forward in response to the obvious disrespect. I put my palm against his chest to hold him back. When he meets my eyes, I give a subtle shake of my head. This is politics, not personal. I know how to handle this, but it will require my mate to keep his cool. Max takes a deep breath and I hear his voice in my head.

Just say the word and I will remove his fucking head. No one gets to treat you like that, not even a fucking Alpha. If this is how this pack is run, Jack and the triplets will never meet their family if I have any say.

I give him a smile, grateful to know that he has my back and won't try to overrule me when it comes to my position. This is the kind of partner I need as a prince of the vampire kingdoms. Turning back to the man on the stairs, I let my walls down a little bit so that my power can leak out. Every vampire has an aura of power, but I'm a fucking Sullivan and a Ramos. I am fucking royalty by blood and right. My relatives rule the Americas from the Arctic Circle to the southern-most pebble in Chile.

"Who the fuck are *you* to tell my mate where he can and cannot be in relation to me?" I demand. "Who gave you the right to disrespect me and my mate after you requested our assistance? Bring me your Alpha!"

The man on the stairs flinches but doesn't bother to hide his anger and distaste when he responds. "My Alpha has better things to do than pander to a fucking leech and his guard dog."

The mother fucking audacity of this bitch! I know my mouth is hanging open in shock, but what in the actual fuck?! His words are tantamount to a damned declaration of war. If my uncle or my father were here, his head would be ripped from his body and the entire pack disbanded immediately.

I didn't think people this fucking stupid really existed outside of books and television. I found a fucking unicorn of dumbassery and stupidity.

While I am frozen in my sheer dumbfounded-ness, Max shifts into his wolf and pounces on the man, snarling in his face. His white wolf has him pinned easily and his growl echoes through the neighborhood. The smell of urine finally shakes me from my stupor, and I notice that the idiot pissed himself in terror.

Serves him right, Max sends to me. *He's a liability to his pack.*

"We can't kill him for being a dumbass," I sigh out loud, only half attempting to hide me regret, as I approach the giant wolf. His head reaches my shoulder, so I lay my arm across his wide body, burying my fingers in the snowy fur. It's softer than I expected...

Max makes a show of backing off the man while people are rushing outside from the surrounding homes. The massive wolf even sneers and sneezes at the the puddle beneath the man. I can't hold back the laugh that bursts from my mouth. Apparently, Ethan isn't the only wolf I know who can broadcast snark in wolf form. As if to prove my point, Max licks up the entire side of my face.

"Ugh, seriously?" I grimace as I use the bottom of my shirt to wipe off the slobber. "You aren't a Saint Bernard! Professionalism please... at least until we're back at the hotel."

I give the wolf a little hip check while I finish wiping. When I lower my shirt, there are new people in the doorway of the house staring at us with looks mixed with horror and hope. Wait – they're staring at my mate, not us.

39

MAX

My wolf wants to teach the sad excuse for a man on the stairs more of a visceral lesson, but I have to remind him that this is not our pack and if we harm one of their members, the Alpha here would be within his rights take it out on Josh. My wolf eventually relents when he recognizes another scent in the air. After teasing josh with a giant lick, he focuses our attention on the door to the house in front of us.

When it opens, I feel like I've fallen through an alternate dimension. The man is almost the carbon copy of Aaron, my mentor and Ms. Anna's younger brother. There are subtle differences, like age lines and the man in front of me is less broad, but with more force behind his aura. The woman is easily over six foot herself, with mocha skin and kind charcoal eyes. My wolf is calling out to them, jumping around inside of me like a puppy...

No.

This can't be possible.

Josh's fingers tighten in my fur and I glance up to him. He looks between me and the couple in front of us. His eyes are glassy, and he offers me a smile. I can see pain in his eyes, but I don't know what is causing it.

You're home, Max, he sends to me mentally. *I'll give you guys some time.*

Then he's gone. Fucking vampire speed!

I turn in the direction I can scent that he ran and want to take off after him, but my wolf stops me.

Family, he tells me. *Pack.*

As much as I need to stop my mate from running away, I owe it to myself to find out exactly what is going on here. Josh said he's giving me some time. He didn't say goodbye.

Trust mate, my wolf tells me. Yeah, buddy. I trust him. I just don't trust these strangers in front of me.

I trot back over to the car and position myself next to the trunk before I shift back to human form. As shifters, we don't generally have an issue with nudity, but these people are strangers and my mate isn't around. They don't get to see me that way. I open the trunk and pull out a pair of basketball shorts from my bag, glad I threw a few in as a precaution.

When I slam the trunk, I see the woman bend over to grab the man on the stairs by the ear, yanking him up onto his feet. "What do you mean that was the fucking prince?! Do you know what you've done, you stupid fucking prick?!"

"Sweetheart," the larger man puts his hand on the woman who is apparently his mate's shoulder. "We still have a guest. Please refrain from killing your cousin's mate in front of company."

I snort a small laugh at their reactions. At least this couple seems to understand the gravity of the dumbass's insults. Their response gives me some hope that Jackie and the triplets would be safe here if I ever have to take them away from the Jameson Pack. I can keep Ms. Anna's promise with an easy heart as long as people like these two are the ones in charge.

When I head back toward the house, the woman throws the piss soaked man to the arms of some warriors who have approached from the lake behind the house. Where the fuck were they while he was out here courting war?

"Take his ass to the cellar," she commands them. "And Jonas? You *will* report as to where you and your men were when James here decided to insult the *FUCKING VAMPIRE REGENT* when we specifically invited him here."

"And his mate," I cough out. The couple on the steps look at me in surprise before managing to mask it. A few of the warriors don't hide their sneers as they glance at my neck. I release a growl and they all look away. Fucking cowards. Except the couple... They seem to be happy about it.

"And his mate," the man in the doorway repeats with force, still looking at me with a smile. "It seems like fate has brought us more than we asked for today, so the gathering planned for two weeks from now will be moved up to tomorrow. This month, we celebrate the new moon. Spread the word."

As the warriors drag off the trembling mess that I can only assume is James, the woman steps out and announces in a voice ringing with authority, "And if I hear any of you say or do a single thing to this man or his mate that is anything other than welcoming, you will face *ME* in the training grounds."

Up and down the street, doors slam as the people rush back inside. The free show is apparently over and announcements were made. I raise my eyebrow at the couple in the doorway. We are the only ones still outside, but I am certain there are ears pressed to doors and windows cracked in all directions. The woman looks like she is on the verge of tears, but the man is rubbing the back of his neck. It's like being in a time machine. Aaron used to do that when his sister would rip him a new one.

"Can I hug you?" the woman blurts out, bouncing on the balls of her feet. "Wait – that's a weird thing to just blurt out, right? But I didn't know you were still alive. Oh, my gods, you must hate us..."

The confusion must show on my face because the man pulls her into his side and whispers in her ear. I don't know if he meant for me to hear it, but my hearing has always been better than most.

"Hush, Maria. Can't you see he is confused? I am pretty sure he didn't come here for us." There is an undertone of sadness in his voice. "Our son is alive. That is enough to be thankful for. Hoping for him to accept us might be asking too much."

"Your *son*?!" I shout, backing toward the car. "Who the fuck is your son? I am Maximillian Andrew Stephens, head warrior of the

Jameson Pack, and I was sent here as an escort to my mate, Prince Joshua Javier Sullivan."

I watch their faces as I back away. This isn't right. This can't be. My mother told me she didn't know who my father was. My mother... isn't my mother.

I stop moving and look up at the face of the woman in front of me. My mother always said I took after my father. That's why I didn't have her gray eyes or light hair. Looking into these charcoal eyes, I finally allow myself to start believing it. The woman who raised me isn't my mother. This woman in front of me is.

"We were going to name you Andrew," she whimpers before burying her face in her mate's shoulder.

"This isn't a discussion we should be having in the driveway," the man says with a glance up the street. Curtains flutter in windows on either side. "Let's take this into my office. Maximillian Stephens, head warrior of the Jameson pack, you and your mate are forever and always welcome in the Snowden pack."

The authority of his last statement rings through the pack bonds and my wolf howls in agreement and joy inside of me. I'm still struggling to accept it, but my wolf has no doubts. These people are my birth parents. But why didn't they raise me?

"Just Max, please. Can I... May I have my mate join me?" I pause before I enter the house. I can't face this without Josh. These people are strangers. If it was just about Jackie and the babies, or even Ethan, I could handle it alone. But this is my own heart. I can't face this without my other half.

"Of course, sweetie," the woman, Maria, answers with a watery smile. I can't think of her as my mother yet. That word has too many negative associations for me. "Do you need to call him? Did you lose your phone in your shift?"

I shake my head when she holds out her own phone and close my eyes.

Baby? Can you come back? I send to him, hoping he kept our connection open. *I need you. I can't face them without you.*

40

JOSH

I ran to a gazebo in one of the national parks in the area. I've spent some time around here when we visited Uncle Edward's kingdom as a family growing up. Everyone else visited us to go to Disneyland and Hollywood, but Mama knew I always preferred a balance between nature and the industrial. I think that's why she pushed Uncle Edward to choose me over my older siblings.

The eastern kingdom has some of the most beautiful nature without sacrificing the convenience and technology of the modern world. And it isn't so separated that you have to choose ahead of time which one you want to experience. In the span of an hour, you can go from being surrounded by skyscrapers to being surrounded by miles upon miles of forest.

You can't get that out west, not really. You have to commit to hours in a car usually to just escape the cities and the scenery outside of the national parks is just all the same... flat. At least Uncle Patrick has the mountains, but his kingdom has the opposite issue. It's too much nature, not enough cities.

I ran off to give Max a chance to learn the truth himself. I really tried not to listen in, but the woman's thoughts were louder than a goal announcer for international futbol. *Uncle Reynaldo would slap me silly if he heard me refer to it as soccer.*

Of course, the woman recognized her long lost son and wants to reconnect. He has her eyes, and now it is painfully obvious why he has that delicious color of skin. The family resemblance is painfully obvious when you put the two of them in the same space. Max deserves to know a mother's love without it being tainted by how they feel about his being mated to a vampire.

Baby? Can you come back? I need you. I can't face this without you.

I take a deep breath and debate for about a minute if there is an excuse I can give him to not go. Of course, I dismiss that idea once I realize what I'm doing. If my mate needs me, I have to be there. Even if they treat me like dogshit, I will be there for him.

It takes less than ten seconds to get back to the car where Max is standing in just a pair of shorts. Scoffing at his lack of modesty, I open the trunk to dig a shirt out of his bag. He turns at the sound and proceeds to get a face full of the t-shirt I throw at his head. When he pulls it on, I laugh at the photo on the front. It's obvious Ethan picked it out, and I'm ninety five percent certain that it was not meant to be packed, let alone worn in the company of another pack's Alpha couple.

Following my gaze, my mate looks down and chuckles at the unicorn leaping across the front of the shirt, glittery rainbows flowing out of its ass. I sigh with a smile and close the trunk to walk over next to him. Taking his hand, we face the front door where his mother throws back her head in laughter. His father actually runs into the doorframe in his haste to get inside. A few seconds later, there is a very loud bark of laughter from deeper inside the house.

I glance up to Max's face with a smile which he returns with a tentative one of his own as we walk up the steps and into the house behind his mother, Maria. We follow her until we come to a door labeled conference room where she asks us to wait a moment. She slips inside and the soundproofing must be good because I can't hear anything, nor can I listen in using my psychic abilities. When she comes back out, Max raises an eyebrow and she chuckles.

"My father used to have that look," she says as she turns toward the room at the end of the hall. "It stopped working on me when I was twelve and developed a look of my own. My cousins called it *"the mom look."*

"As for that," she says indicating back at the room she just left, "I was asking the Neeley family to come back tomorrow. I know they want answers, but they also deserve everyone's complete attention."

She opens the door marked "Office" and waves us in, not noticing Max's hand tightening in mine or the increase of my heartbeat at the mention of Erica's family.

The room we enter appears cozy. The only indication that it is an office is a small desk in front of a wall of filing cabinets. Even the desk only holds a laptop and a tray for mail. It is nothing like any pack or clan or coven leader's office I've ever been in, and my family has ensured I have seen a lot.

"Welcome to the Snowden pack," Maria says waving us over to the sitting area. "I'm getting something to drink. It's after noon, right?"

We all look at the clock on the wall as the minute hand shifts to one minute past twelve. That seems to be the last string of tension that needed to be cut for me and I collapse onto one of the sofas with minimal grace. Max sits gingerly next to me, still not able to relax. I thread my fingers back through his to grasp his sweaty palm in mine and lean against his shoulder.

"Just a soda for me," I tell her with a smile. "Sprite if you have it, but I'm not picky as long as it isn't diet. Artificial sweeteners are not my thing."

"Are you sure?" the Alpha enters the room and sits on the sofa opposite us. "I have a nice blood wine that we keep on hand for when the other vampire delegates visit."

My smile freezes on my face and my breath stops. I have to remind myself: *They don't know about the blood. They are being nice and courteous...* I feel Max's arm come around my shoulders and I can breathe again.

"Just the soda," he says. "For both of us."

Thank you, I send to him and he squeezes my side in response. I know they will know about my issue soon enough, but Erica's family deserves to hear it from me before their Alpha does. It's the only courtesy I have to offer them at this point.

When Maria comes back in with our drinks: coffee for the Alpha, sodas for the two of us, and a pint glass of what smells like scotch for her, Max opens up the discussion with addressing the elephant in the room.

"So," he says taking a swig from his glass, "how did I end up in the hands of the wicked bitch of the west?"

The Alpha spits coffee to the side, and the white chair in the corner now looks like little Alec had one of his infamous explosions on it. Maria chugs her scotch like it's apple juice. I even take an extra sniff to make sure I wasn't mistaken regarding what was in the glass. Nope – it is straight up scotch with a hint of wolfsbane. She is going to be feeling that later.

I hand the box of tissues from the table over to the Alpha. He gives me a look of gratitude before trying to wipe his face. Maria finishes off her glass and gets up to refill it with whatever is on the cart in the corner of the office. I can feel the pettiness radiating from my mate and I reach under our joined hands to pinch him on the leg.

Behave! You don't know how they felt seeing you. They wanted you.

He looks at me with pain and rage in his eyes. *Then why was I with that woman? Why was she able to do those things? Why did no one look for me or find me? Why didn't Ms. Anna know who my parents were? She was obviously related to the Alpha here, so why was I abandoned there?*

The Alpha seems to be the first to regain his composure and he responds to Max's original question. "Considering we were told you died at the hospital, we don't know who raised you," he says with obvious pain. "We tried for so long to get answers, but the doctors insisted that you never took your first breath. The nurse who took you from the room died in a car accident that same day, so we never found out what happened to your body."

"We assumed it was sold to the demons and it caused decades of animosity between our races," Maria adds when she sits back down. "Because of the tensions, even King Edward avoids coming here unless specifically requested. He was here for mediation almost a decade ago, but when they refused to take responsibility, talks broke down and only his threats to destroy all of us kept us from going to war."

"That's when the demons moved out of Michigan and Ohio," I whisper as the pieces are coming together. Everyone in the room is silent with my interruption, but I can't stop my mouth. "That's why the lab could set up without detection. The closest wolf pack was run by a self-centered bewitched imbecile and the demons moved southeast. The next closest packs were here and Ellicott City. The closest witch coven would have been Nashville, and my uncle avoided Ohio because of Ethan..."

I look at Max in horror and awe at the revelation. It was fucking brilliant... diabolical, but brilliant. "That asswipe demigod prick knew there was no one to stop him!"

"Good job, Sherlock," says a woman's voice from over by the drink cart and we all jump. There is a tiny girl, woman, female presenting person of indeterminate age, standing there with a smug look on her face. "That family fucked up so many timelines just to try and stop what they ultimately caused."

She pours herself a couple fingers of scotch and turns back to face us all, leaning on the wall with her neon pink mohawk swaying side to side as she hums something too quiet for us to notice. I pop into her head, only to hear that damn nursery song and jump out, physically jumping into Max's lap.

Holy shit!

"Cassie?" I ask with a gulp. Her answering smirk is enough of an answer for me. This is one of the fucking fates! Not only one of them, but the one who has made it her personal mission to fuck around with Ethan and his family to fix what that damn bitch of a goddess broke.

She slams back the rest of her scotch with a grimace. "I know you need it to get a buzz, but why do you wolves ruin the good stuff with aconite? Spike the rot-gut, not the singe malt."

"Anyways," she says as she flops into the coffee-stained chair. "I guess I can fill you guys in on what happened back then since all

153

responsible parties are dead and my favorite boy isn't here to channel them."

She flicks her hand at the wall and a hovering movie screen appears. The scene playing on it looks like a movie from the nineties, but I realize quickly, it's a memory from no one's perspective. Is this what the fates see?

How the fuck do they stay sane?

"We don't," Cassie says with a wave of her hand, answering my silent question. "Popcorn anyone?"

We all stare at her as she stuffs her face with the bowl of popcorn that appeared from nothing. With another snap of her fingers, the light in the room dims and our attention is pulled back to the scene she is playing for us all.

41

MAX

My brain can barely wrap around the fact that I am sitting in the room with my birth parents who apparently thought I was dead all this time. Now, the fucking fate bestie of Ethan has shown up to apparently reveal what happened back then. I mean, they aren't really best friends, but Ethan has a ton of respect for her and what she's done for his family. She saved all of us by making sure key players were in the right places.

My attention is pulled to the screen she conjured up when I hear a woman screaming.

"Alvin! You are never coming near my vagina again!" she screams as sweat pours from her skin. Her dark curls are matted to her forehead as her mate wipes her brow with a rag.

"Anything you say, Love," he croons before wincing as the sound of bones cracking fills the room. I glance at his hand and notice at least three fingers are bent in the wrong direction.

It takes a second to reconcile that the two people on the screen are the same as the couple sitting across from me. Does this mean that I'm watching my birth?

"One more big push," the nurse says from between Maria's legs. "Your boy is almost out."

Maria screams and the moment the baby slides out of her is obvious from the way her body relaxes. The nurse cuts the cord and turns away to clean the baby and clear his airway. Another nurse replaces her and starts guiding Maria through expelling the placenta while our view follows the first nurse.

"He's not breathing," the nurse mutters to the room and rushes out of the room, clutching the baby to her as she runs down the hallway. At the elevator, she pushes the down button but no one pays attention when the doors open.

"But the NICU was the floor above delivery," Maria mutters from in front of me.

The nurse hits the button labeled M and the doors close. As the elevator drops, the baby in her arms starts to cry. The woman holding him has tears in her own eyes as she whispers to him. "I'm so sorry, baby boy. She says I can have my baby if you're raised in another pack. I'm sure you'll be loved. Your parents are so amazing, there is no way you won't be."

The doors open and the nurse wipes under her eyes and carries the baby into the morgue with her head held high. Inside, there are three people waiting. They turn when the nurse carries the baby inside.

Josh whimpers and clutches my hand tighter. I look between him and the screen and realize I recognize all three of the people waiting for the baby, for me. One is the fucking goddess that screwed us all over. The other woman is the bitch who raised me and lied to me my whole life. The third one is a man – significantly younger, but still an adult. It's the douchebag demigod so-called doctor who was behind the lab and all of the shit that went down there.

The nurse hesitates before placing the baby into the carrier sitting on the autopsy table. "And you will let me have this child and raise him or her how I see fit without interference from you or your family?" she asks with her hand on her lower abdomen. "You will be no contact with me or my child for as long as he is unaware of the identity of his father?"

"Of course," the goddess says in a sickly sweet voice. "As long as you are with him, he will be invisible to the remainder of his family. My word as a goddess cannot be questioned."

"While he is unaware of his father's true identity," the nurse insists, holding the baby more securely. "I'm not leaving it open for you to arrange my death and steal my child. Swear it! Or this baby goes nowhere."

She takes a device out of her pocket and the screen zooms in on it to show there is an emergency button on it. "I press this button and the hospital goes into lockdown and you go nowhere. Give me your word that you agree to my stipulations. All of you! Swear it!"

"I swear it," the goddess sneers.

"Yes, yes," the asswipe says looking like he's in a rush to get out of there.

"Nothing will keep me from my child," says the she-wolf next to the carrier. There is a crazed look on her face, but the nurse doesn't notice while she kisses the baby on the forehead.

"Please forgive me, sweet babe," she whispers. "I hope my child has the opportunity to make this up to you someday. I'm so sorry."

She places the baby in the carrier and runs from the room in tears.

The scene freezes and the lights come up. I glance over at my parents and see a mix of anger and compassion on their faces. I just feel numb. I was taken away from these people for some reason that I cannot fathom. That nurse was just a mother trying to save her own child. For whatever reason, the goddess had a say in the child being born...

"What happened to her baby?" I ask Cassie since no one else is talking.

The fate looks at me in confusion, like I surprised her by wanting to know. Nice to know that even the fates can't see everything.

"I don't see how people feel," she answers my unspoken thought. "As for her kid, he grew up and found out who his father is eventually. His story is still being fixed, though. He wasn't even supposed to exist."

Josh tenses in my lap before asking, "Does that mean you have to kill him to fix the timeline?"

Cassie laughs before shoveling more popcorn into her mouth. Mumbling around her chewing, she responds saying, "This isn't Supernatural and they didn't unsink the Titanic. It just means weaving him into someone else's fate. I met Ethan too late to weave him in there since his and Alaric's bond was already established. But I didn't forget him. I've set things in motion for the little demi-demon.

"But back to the movie," she says sitting up straight in the chair, showing obvious excitement. "This is the best part!"

The she-wolf picks up the infant carrier and holds it in front of her face. She is smiling at the baby like he is her entire world.

"As promised," the demigod man says to her. "A baby to replace the son you failed to birth for your mate."

"I didn't fail!" she yells at him.

That voice makes me cringe now. I spent my entire life hearing that voice screeching at me – demanding money, booze, drugs, food... Whatever she craved, she expected me to get it for her or do what she wanted so she could get it. I spent most of my years dependent on that voice while fearing it at the same time.

She swings the carrier dangerously as she stomps out of the morgue. Before the view follows her, the goddess turns to the demigod man and says, "This will drive a wedge between the Alpha couple so that my chosen one can take her place as the true power in that pack. Our glory and victory over the other races is almost assured. Just don't disobey me again. I won't clean up your mistakes again. You know the gods of our family can't reproduce without my blessing. You destroyed that she-wolf's mind by impregnating her."

The man laughs coldly before replying, "You know I had to do it, Auntie. Scientifically, it was necessary to see the effect of stillbirth in a she-wolf. I've already witnessed miscarriages and infertility and how it affects mates."

"But she has no mate," the goddess says as they head for the door. "She is unmarked."

"Ah, but she thinks her lover is her mate," he says as he shifts his appearance to a dark skinned man closely resembling a twenty something athlete. Dropping the glamour, he adds, "She will never find him again, and I can observe whether emotions or biology is a stronger factor when it comes to child rearing."

"You have broken her mind and torn her soul," the goddess looks at her nephew in revulsion.

He doesn't seem to notice as he leaves the room in front of her. She sighs in exasperation, but ultimately follows him out of the room.

42

JOSH

As the scene cuts off, the lights come on and the screen disappears. I turn to look at Cassie, but there is no sign that she was here at all. She even cleaned up her popcorn mess and the coffee spray from the chair. I shimmy off Max's lap to sit next to him again and we share a confused glance.

"So... that's Cassie," my mate says to his clearly confused parents. "She kind of helped us in a battle we had with the gods last month, and I guess she's making it a point to keep in touch?"

I giggle-snort and slap my hands over my mouth in mortification. This is not the impression I want to be making on my in-laws.

Maria laughs at my outburst and goes to refill her glass again, reaching under the cart for a different crystal decanter. When she opens it, the smell of a quality single malt scotch fills the room, no hint of wolfsbane.

"Nice to know the fates aren't omniscient," she says as she pours herself and her mate a few fingers each. "With the way she eats, this would have been wasted on her."

Max and the Alpha both laugh at that as Maria resumes her seat next to her mate. We all sit for a few minutes in silence, thinking over what we all just sat through. I've taken a dive into memories before, so it's not quite so bad for me. I know Max has seen some of Ethan's through his nightmares, so he recovered rather quickly himself. The Alpha couple seems to need a little push.

I clear my throat to get everyone's attention. "Now that you all have had a chance to think it over, are there any pressing questions?" I ask as I look at each of them in turn. "Max? Alpha? Ms. Maria?"

Maria winces when I get to her and waves off my look of concern.

"I want to tell you boys to call me Mom, but I understand another woman has had that privilege and it stings," she says hurriedly. "Just ignore the pre-menopausal she-wolf and continue."

"She wasn't Mom," my mate says softly, gripping my hand too tightly to let me believe he is alright. "She was Mommy when I was too young to know better, but she was never a mom. I have referred to that woman only as my mother, purely from an identification stand-point, from the time I was six years old and she sold my body for the first time."

It feels like the universe pauses for a second before the Alpha and his mate explode from their seats talking over each other about how they will hunt her down and do some rather creative things to the woman. Halfway through, Maria switches to Spanish and I will totally assist her if she wants to pursue what she is talking about doing.

I accidentally snort my Sprite because of one of Maria's suggestions and my resultant coughing fit seems to break through the tension in the room. They both sit back down in a huff while I am struggling to clear my airway from the carbonation. They are still breathing a bit heavy, but at least they didn't shift.

Max barely glances at them before focusing back on me, rubbing my back gently. "She wasn't always bad," he says, still looking at me. "Seeing that last part helped put the pieces together for me. Until her wolf noticed the truth, she was a wonderful mother, and I had an amazing, but stern, grandmother. The woman left behind when Gran passed was broken. That woman remained broken. As long as I was alive and in front of her, her wolf could never escape the pain of losing her child and her mate. Fake as it was, her wolf was always in mourning...

"It's only been in the last few years that she has found peace..."

He lowers his forehead to my shoulder, and I wrap my arms around him. How the fuck can he be so gracious? That woman abused the hell out of him and yet he's relieved that she is at peace and happy somewhere.

I love you so much.

He raises his eyes to meet mine for a second and I see his heart reflected back to me. He doesn't need to say it back. I mean, well... I would love to hear it, but I can see it. I don't deserve someone this purely good.

"That fucking woman doesn't deserve peace," the Alpha mutters before getting slapped on the back of his head. Maria glares at him before turning back to us.

"What changed for her?" she asks.

Max takes a deep breath and sits back up to look at them. "She met her fated mate and forgot I exist," he says.

43

MAX

My mate wraps his arms around me and buries his face in my chest. The couple across from me grasp each other's hands as tears start to stream down Maria's cheeks. She covers her mouth in shock, probably wondering how a mother could forget her own child. I pondered that a lot myself when I left her behind in Mississippi.

Now, I know the reason. I was never her child. I was a physical reminder for her wolf that she had been pregnant and it put her constantly on edge as I grew and my looks and scent didn't match the image in her memories. Her wolf knew something was wrong, and the woman needed the drugs and alcohol to keep her wolf dulled.

"Knowing the truth," I tell them as I lift Josh's gaze to meet mine, "it actually helps to make it hurt a helluva lot less. She was in pain every day from the time that asshole tricked her into sleeping with him. *She lost a fucking child* and was not given the chance to mourn. Her wolf didn't get to mourn her pup because the human half was convinced that the pup never died."

Turning my full attention to my mate, I explain it more fully. The others in the room would understand what it means when the human and wolf are at odds, but as far as I'm aware, vampires don't have an equivalent.

"When a pup is a baby, they smell kind of pure, like fresh snow or sunshine or some intangible thing that is like the embodiment of goodness. Think of how the triplets scent for a reference. As they get older, they start to scent like their family. By the age of five or so, the pup will carry the scents of its parents. I just didn't realize that it was a genetic thing and not just repeated exposure before today."

"Actually," Alpha Alvin cuts in. "I was unaware it was biological as well. We will have to update the records and get word out to the other packs to make sure everyone is aware. We don't need other children suffering because of their parentage."

"Can you let him explain this to his mate before you go all Alpha, ya dumb fuck?" Maria says as she slaps her mate on the arm. "Read the fucking room, will ya?"

It is getting easier by the minute to accept this woman as my birth mother. I can see where I get my sense of humor and attitude.

"For an example of the family scent thing," I continue, turning back to Josh to explain, "Ethan scented like Connor's family, but I contributed the differences in their scents to the fact that Connor already had his wolf by the time I met them both. Ethan scented as related to Connor, so no one questioned it. We didn't know they were only cousins and not brothers until just this last year."

Josh nods like he's following along. I glance over to the people who created me, and see that they are confused, but they indicate I should continue in my explanation for my mate. I'll fill them in on Ethan later.

"So, when my scent started coming in right around the time Gran died, her wolf knew I wasn't her baby. The wolf likely started to demand she go searching for her baby or to return me to my rightful family. Either way, the human side of her believed I was truly the baby she had with her mate while the wolf knew the truth.

"The wolf is usually submissive to the human side, but sometimes when there is conflict the wolf can overpower the human. Looking back, I can think of a few instances where that might have happened. The last time I can remember, I was about seven or eight. It was shortly after..."

I shiver and Josh gives me a squeeze to let me know I don't have to say it. Even with the years of therapy, I still struggle to let it out, to not feel dirty because of it.

"Anyways, she took me to the bus depot in Dayton and pointed to a map, telling me to go to where she was pointing before she left me there. I was too small and too scared. I didn't see where she pointed. A policeman saw me crying all alone and called the emergency contact number sewn into my backpack. He called Ms. Anna and she picked me up and brought me home."

Josh wraps his arms around my neck and climbs back fully into my lap to give me comfort that I desperately need. My savior, my angel, inadvertently gave me back to my abuser at that time.

"After that, she kept the wolf subdued with drugs and alcohol almost all of the time. I thought she stopped caring completely, but she wasn't totally evil under that spell. She still protected me from the fae when they came into our house looking for Alpha Dick."

I lay a kiss on Josh's forehead and rest my chin on his shoulder. "Knowing what I know, she did her best all things considered. Thankfully, Dick refused to let her move with the rest of the pack to South Carolina when he was running away from his guilt, so I did the dutiful son thing and found her a new pack. The Alpha in Mississippi was the only one of the Eastern Alpha Alliance who was willing to even meet us thanks to her reputation as a whore."

"Ironically enough," I say, resting my head back against the back of the sofa, "When she opened her door to get out of the car, her true mate scented her and vice versa."

Sitting up straight, I stare at the table in front of me. "He's a beta who works as an accountant for their pack with a lovely two bedroom home and three cats. It was like seeing the sun burn through the fog. The woman I spent eighteen years with disappeared before my eyes, and she was free.

"I was free," I say much softer, only for my mate. He would understand where the people on the other sofa would not. Her forgetting me was the greatest gift she could ever grant me. My last tie to her was severed, and I was no longer responsible for her.

"Her new Alpha has promised to inform me if she ever slips up or they decide to leave his pack, but now I think they are right where they are supposed to be," I say as I lean back in my seat to look at my parents. "I think Cassie is working to get all of us back to where we are supposed to be."

The Alpha murmurs in agreement while Maria is nodding with a soft smile. They give each other a look before the man I now know is my father decides to ask another question.

"Son," he says with a smile. "Does your Ms. Anna have a white wolf?"

44

MAX

Holy fuck! Ms. Anna was my aunt! I still can't believe it.

Alpha Alvin, my father, was devastated to find out she passed away about eight years ago. Apparently, Alpha Dick made her cut off contact with her family when he marked her. Alvin didn't even know what pack she was mated in to, only that her new Alpha was horribly inclusionary. Their younger brother Aaron went to search for her when it was obvious she wasn't returning from her year of wandering to look for her mate.

When Aaron sent word that he found Anna, everyone was overjoyed until his next message came through saying she found her mate and would not be returning. Outsiders were not welcome, and he was joining the pack to keep watch over their sister.

They never even knew Ric was born, let alone Jack. They didn't know about the car accident. They didn't know Ms. Anna had died. They had been triplets, and Alvin had no idea he was the only one left alive. I watched my father grieve for his siblings, his litter mates, almost a decade later all because my own Alpha's father was too much of a dick to meet his in-laws. I made the offer to have Ric contact them, but Alpha Alvin said he wants to sleep on what he's learned before he commits to anything.

After dinner, my parents excused themselves for the night, so Josh and I headed to the suite they offered to us. We are getting ready for bed in the guest suite instead of going back to the hotel out of courtesy. They argued that there is no reason to stay in a hotel when we are all family. I was still ready to refuse, but Josh tugged on my arm and I realized he was exhausted from all of the emotions. To be honest, so am I.

Pulling back the covers on the queen size bed, I realize I am going to either have my feet hanging off the edge of the bed or I'm going to have to be diagonal across the entire bed. At least the king size in the hotel wasn't too bad as long as I was propped up on enough pillows.

"What to you say to being diagonal in the bed?" I ask Josh as he starts to climb in. His look of perplexion makes me smile. "I'm too tall for a queen."

"Not for this queen," he mumbles before slapping his hands over his mouth.

I chuckle and climb over the bed so I can put my head in the corner near him, leaving my feet pointed to the corner on the side I started on. Patting the bed to the inside of my body, I indicate he needs to climb over me to get in. He makes me laugh outright as he makes the attempt without removing his hands from covering his mouth. I finally give in and pull him down myself, eliciting a squeak from behind his hands.

I yank the covers up and over us and reach over to flip the switch on the lamp on the bedside table. Josh stops me before I can turn it off, and I look at him. He looks nervous.

"Can we leave it on? Or maybe the bathroom light?" he asks.

He doesn't need to elaborate. Having been in his memory, I won't subject him to the darkness if he doesn't want it. I pull him closer and place a gentle kiss on his temple. "Anything you want, Little One."

45

JOSH

I know it's stupid. I had zero issue last night in the hotel when it came to having the lights off. But last night, the curtains on the window were sheer and the light from outside was able to come in. This room has blackout curtains. *"Put in just for the comfort of our occasional nocturnally configured guests."* Maria had said as she showed us the suite. Not like I need another reminder that I'm a reject when it comes to being a vampire.

I can't drink blood. I am afraid of the dark.

I'm a freak.

"Do you really love me?" I whisper on a breath, knowing Max has to be asleep by now. There is no possible way he can still want someone as messed up as me after finding out that not only is he an Alpha Heir, he's also blood related to his angel. Not only that, his found family is actually his blood family so he doesn't have to be conflicted about how he feels about them anymore.

"Nothing in the universe will ever make me stop loving you," his voice whispers back to me. I startle in his arms at the sound and he gives me a squeeze. "You need to stop asking me when you think I can't hear you."

"How can you love me?" I ask him honestly. "I'm so fucked up. I can't possibly make you happy. I'll only tear you down, like your mother did... or rather, like the woman who raised you did."

Max sits up and pulls me up onto his lap facing him so that we are eye to eye. "You listen to me, Joshua Javier Sullivan," He growls out, gripping my chin tightly. "You are a kind and caring and overly empathetic person. You love when you shouldn't. You trust when you should be wary. You sacrifice when you have nothing left. You are nothing like that woman, neither before, during, nor after her curse from that douchebag.

"You are *mine*. I will never let you go. And the only reason you don't yet bear my mark is because I don't want to cause you unnecessary pain by drawing your blood for the bite."

Something inside of me snaps and I reach for his face. Cupping my palms on his cheeks, I delight in the feel of his stubble on my skin. Vampires have to make a conscious decision to grow hair or age once they freeze into their immortality as long as they feed on blood or another magical source. With my ability to feed on light, I haven't had to shave since I was fifteen, and that peach fuzz was honestly just wishful thinking.

I rub my hands back and forth, relishing the scratch of the hairs prickling against my palms. I want to feel this sensation somewhere a bit further south, but I need to get my thoughts out before little Josh decides he's running the show. I don't mean little like how my cousin gets, but rather like the appendage in my pants that has decided it will take over if I don't hurry the fuck up.

"I want to wear your mark," I tell Max as I lean in to give him a gentle peck on the lips. "But first, I want you to eat my ass and give me beard burn. Fuck me into the mattress and mark me as yours, inside and out."

He searches my eyes and when he sees no fear, I swear I can hear his wolf howl in joy as Max's eyes shift from charcoal to ice blue for a split second. I have zero reservations in this moment. There is only anticipation and a sense of peace from the rightness of my decision.

46

MAX

If someone would have asked me hours ago if I would be willing to do anything sexual in my newly discovered parents' house, I would have said they were insane. If the possibility of Josh letting me mark him tonight had even remotely entered my mind as a possibility, I would have insisted we go back to the hotel.

I guess this day is nothing but surprises.

Flipping my mate around, I rip his sleep shorts away. Fuck it. He should have something in his bag to cover up in the morning. Seeing no underwear for the second day in a row, I am starting to wonder if he prefers to go commando or if he just forgot to pack underwear. I'll ask in the morning because I do believe my mate requested some beard burn in a rather unforgettable place.

Giving his perfect globes a squeeze, I chuckle. There's the noise I want to hear from my mate. Josh tries to raise himself up on his knees so that he can muffle his mouth with his hands, but I push back him down with one hand between his shoulder blades. His forehead is on the bed between my calves with his shoulders resting on my knees. His hands are clamped tightly over his mouth, and I am determined to see if we can embarrass the people who brought me into this world.

Catching your kid having sex is like a rite of passage, right?

Before I let myself get distracted, I dive back down between mate's ass cheeks to begin my feast. I want to take my time with this.

47

JOSH

Can a vampire die from too many orgasms? Asking for reasons...

My body won't stop moving on its own as Max leans back against the headboard. I never thought of myself as a twitchy o-man, but based on the last twenty four hours with my mate, I think I need to reevaluate a lot of assumptions about my body and sex.

"I'm dead," I mumble into the mattress between Max's legs. "You've discovered how to kill a vampire without removing his head."

Hell, I think he removed everything *from* my head, at least the one down there. Actually, the one up here doesn't seem to be firing on all cylinders either. If I had known having someone eat me out would be like that, I might have asked for it way before this. I don't think I can move, even with my mate climbing out from under me, rolling me onto my back to stare at the ceiling.

I hear a weird snapping sound, but I am too blissed out to worry. Max probably wants to brush his teeth again or something. I mean, his tongue was just in an ass. I don't mind it so much since we can't transmit or contract diseases that way with being supernaturals. And I mean, I don't have any functions back there unless I eat human food for a few days straight, but he might care.

I feel something pushing against my backdoor and my eyes fly open. My mate is leaning over me with a smirk, and my brain finally puts it together when two of his fingers are inside of me scissoring and stretching me gently where his tongue had already softened me up before.

Oh... that snap was lube.

Gee, brain... keep up please. This is fucking amazing. Max adds a third finger and I stuff my fist in my mouth to try and keep quiet. It was difficult enough while he was feasting on my ass, but now, I don't have the mattress below me to muffle the sound. I try to reach for a pillow and he kicks them all off the bed, almost knocking the lamp off the side table.

What the fuck? Your parents are going to hear me!

"Let them hear it," he leans down and whispers in my ear. I shiver and have to hold back a scream when he simultaneously finds my prostate and licks my neck, just below my ear.

Please gag me or something! I plead with him without removing my hand. *I can feel my fangs and I don't want to draw blood and ruin this. I want this too much. Please!*

Max pulls back and I feel empty when his fingers leave my hole. I start to worry that he has changed his mind when he jumps back off the bed. But the feeling recedes when I see him coming back tying a knot in one of his t-shirts. When he reaches me, he gently pulls my fist from my mouth, placing a kiss on the bruised knuckles.

"Open wide, Little One," he says as he pushes the knot into my mouth. It stretches my jaw wider than my fist did, but it's not uncomfortable. The cotton is soft as he pulls the end tight to tie it off behind my head. "Still good, baby?"

I nod emphatically before sending my love through the mind link. *Thank you, Love.*

Max presses a kiss to my forehead before grabbing the lube bottle he left on the floor next to the bed. I watch as he coats himself and climbs back into position between my legs. He grabs my thighs and starts to push them into position, bending me practically in half. Using his forearm, he holds me in position by the back of my knees so that he can drizzle some more lube on my hole.

"Don't want you to hurt," he grunts out and tosses the lube toward his bag. "I only want to see pleasure in your eyes."

I feel like my heart is going to explode from pure joy when I finally feel the pressure of him pushing against my entrance. I bear down enthusiastically and he slips inside faster that he apparently is ready for. His arms fall out from under him and he pushes him further inside than either of us is prepared for. The sensation is just slightly on the wrong side of the pain to pleasure scale. I want to hide the fact that it hurts so that he doesn't stop. I don't want to stop.

But Max, showing he understands more than he thinks he does, starts slowly rocking inside of me. He keeps it shallow and slow until I give him a nod to go deeper. He takes his time, going a little bit farther with each thrust until he is sheathed completely in my ass. It could have been minutes or hours, but what I expected to be a rough and primal fucking somehow became soft and gentle love making.

The massage on my prostate lets the pressure build so gradually that my orgasm catches me by surprise. One second, I'm staring into the abyss of love in my mate's eyes, and the next I'm screaming my pleasure to the heavens, held tight against Max's chest while the world explodes. There's a pinching on my neck, but I'm so lost in sensation that the brief wash of pain blends in with the ecstasy as instinct takes over to ride it out.

I come back to myself feeling more secure in my skin than I have probably since before I left California. Licking my lips, the taste explosion makes me hum in delight and I curl into the side of my mate while he strokes my back.

Wait... the taste. My brain is still running slow, but the horror of what I must have done makes me sit up and look at Max's neck. There it is. Two small puncture holes.

Oh, fuck. I drank blood!

I race to the bathroom where I try to throw it up. I want to vomit. I don't want to drink blood. I can't do it! I can't! I promised!

Max crouches down next to me, sitting on the bathroom floor while I spend the next hour dry heaving. He keeps up a string of comforting words, but I don't deserve them. "I'm so sorry, Little One," he keeps saying. He shouldn't apologize to me. It's not his fault that I am a fucking monster.

I don't know how long we stayed there on the floor with me sobbing and him apologizing. I must have passed out at some point because the next thing I know is I am in bed alone, knowing I have to tell Erica's family that I killed her. And now I can't even say that I'd never drank another drop since then.

48

MAX

Coffee is not a luxury after last night, it is a necessity. It went from being the best night of my life to one of the worst, all because I was too fucking selfish, wanting to wear my mate's mark on my neck. I knew he wasn't ready, but he bit through the t-shirt when I marked him and the only thing my wolf wanted was *his* mouth on *us*.

I *know* better than to ask someone to do something mid orgasm. That's how my mother, ugh that woman, got favors from her clients. I swore I would never do that, never take advantage of someone in such a compromised state. But I fucked up. I couldn't sleep for fear that I would wake up to Josh being gone, running from what I made him do.

I'll never get the image out of my head of him trying to force himself to vomit up my blood.

My fault, my wolf supplies. *Blame beast. Mate will forgive man.*

I shake my head while I wait for a cup to pour from the machine. They have the same fancy pod machine that Ethan has, so I at least know how to work it. I open the fridge to see that they have a decent selection of creamers as well. Grabbing the caramel macchiato creamer, I almost drop it when I turn to see the Alpha imitating a zombie on the other side of the room.

"Fucking hell," I mutter as I put my palm to my chest. "My heart gets enough of a workout, thanks very much."

He chuckles dryly before shuffling to the cabinet above the sink to grab out a huge black mug. I don't understand the significance of the mug aside from the size until the hot coffee starts to pour into it. It's one of those color change ones. The hot liquid reveals words that make me snort a laugh: "If you can read this, FUCK OFF. Come back when the coffee is gone." I need to get one of those for Ethan.

"How'd you sleep?" I ask him and have to hold back my laughter when he gives me a look that says "how do you think?"

He takes a sip of his coffee black, and I have to assume I got all my good taste from my mother's side of the family. "I think I might need to invite some witches to visit and improve on the soundproofing spells," he tells me with a smirk and a wink. "Especially if my son and his mate are going to be visiting often."

The smug smile on my face falls as soon as I remember what happened after. The Alpha might be under-caffeinated, but he notices my change in demeanor. When he asks me about it, I try to figure out how much I can say without betraying Josh's story. It is up to him if he wants my parents to know at all, but I know he definitely doesn't want anyone else to know *before* he can talk with the Neeley family.

"I messed up last night," I tell him and he snorts.

"From what we heard before we had to engage the extra sound-proofing on the Alpha suite, you were doing pretty good," he chuckles as he upends his cup setting it back under the machine to brew a second cup. "I take it something happened after?"

For this cup, he goes to the fridge and pulls out the toasted marshmallow creamer and pours some into his coffee. Ah, so my father is like the other Alphas I've met after all. First cup black, *then* they allow themselves to have good tasting stuff. I'll never waste my time like that. Give me good taste over showmanship any day.

Shaking my head, I turn my thoughts back to the conversation at hand. "Josh doesn't drink blood," I tell him and quickly add, "He has his reasons, but it's his choice if you get to know why. It's not my place to decide for him, not even with you."

The Alpha nods solemnly and I continue to explain what happened as best I can. Maybe this would have been more awkward if I had grown up with the man as my father, but right now I just see him as Aaron's older brother. He was my mentor and the closest thing I ever had to a father, so I feel a shadow of that connection with Alvin. Even though the man in front of me is my actual father, in my heart Aaron will always be my first dad.

"In the excitement of marking him, I asked him to mark me," I tell him. "He was so blissed out that he acted on instinct and did." I point to the bite mark on my neck. The injury itself has healed and in its place is a scar to mark me as fully belonging to Josh. "When he came out of the post-O haze, he tasted the blood and panicked. He finally fell asleep on the bathroom floor after hours of dry heaving in his attempt to expel the small amount of my blood that he consumed."

"You poor boys," Maria's voice comes from behind me as she rushes up and hugs me. "Why didn't you say anything about the blood when we kept offering the wine yesterday? We would never want your mate to be uncomfortable or sick just to stand on courtesy."

I give her hands a gentle tap and she releases the hug. I'm not sure I'll ever be able to handle comfort like that, not after how I grew up. Jackie and Ethan get away with it because they have the minds of children. Josh is apparently the only adult who can embrace me without me feeling revulsion. Even Ric any my warriors with the bro-hugs make me tense.

"Like I told your mate," I say with a nod toward the Alpha as I step away from her, "It's up to Josh if you guys will find out his reasons why. He... there is a rather significant series of events that have happened to him in the past and reliving them, even to explain, can be harmful for both him and people around him... If that makes any sense."

My parents exchange a look, and I know they don't understand but are too polite to ask.

"Just say I was held captive and tortured along with about forty other supes for about half a decade and I have some PTSD issues," my mate's voice says from the doorway. "That way we get the pity out of the way so I can leave as soon as the meeting with Erica's family is over."

He moves to the coffee maker and starts a cup with one of the generic mugs hanging next to the machine, just like I did. I get up and grab out the same creamer I used. Josh prefers salted caramel or the girl scout cookie flavors, but this will work enough for him to get by for today. When he sits down on the stool next to mine, he offers me a weak smile in thanks, taking the bottle from me. I watch the light dim in his eyes when his gaze reaches the scar on my neck.

"Who told you the Neeley's daughter's name was Erica?" my father asks, and the creamer bottle falls to the floor.

49

JOSH

Fuck...

I know better than to open my mouth before I have my coffee in the morning. Snark and sarcasm is my default mode until I get caffeine in my system. Add in the emotional hangover and the frustration I could feel from Max trying to explain while keeping my secrets... I was overloaded and forgot that I shouldn't know Erica.

I look at Max in terror. How do I fix this?

"I'm not ready," I tell him, ignoring the Alpha and his mate. "I can't tell them. I have to let her family know first. They deserve that much since I couldn't bring her back."

Max pulls me into his lap and murmurs soothing noises until my breathing evens back out.

"You don't have to tell anyone anything you don't want to," Maria says, coming over to place her hand on my knee. "Sweetie, Alvin was just curious if someone disobeyed his order or if you had information outside of his request."

When I go to open my mouth, my mate covers it with his hand.

"Drink your coffee first," he says with a smile. "Get the caffeine to your brain cells before you talk."

Maria pats my knee and turns to go back to the counter where she set her own coffee, and for the next fifteen minutes, we all sit in the kitchen with only slightly awkward silence filling the room.

"Alright boys," Maria finally says clapping her hands. "I'm making breakfast. Pancakes or waffles?"

Max shrugs and looks to me to decide. I look at the Alpha who mirrors his son and also looks at me. I guess the decision is mine.

"Actually, can you do French toast? If not, that's fine, but my roommate gets a rash from eggs and I miss French toast so much."

Maria bounces on the balls of her feet like Ethan does when he gets excited, and she starts grabbing ingredients before pushing us all out to the sitting room. I can't help but chuckle at how much she reminds me of Mama. I think they might end up friends as long as I'm still welcome after today.

Max pulls me down on his lap on one of the sofas while Alpha Alvin picks up a tablet from the mantle before settling in a massive recliner. This silence isn't awkward at all while we wait for breakfast to be ready.

50

JOSH

"You sure you don't need anything, sweetie?"

I smile and shake my head at Maria for what feels like the hundredth time today. It really is a shame that her and Alvin didn't have any other kids because she's got the mom thing down pat.

"Why didn't you guys have any other babies?" I blurt out while we are waiting in the conference room for Erica's family to show up. "You have this huge house, but it's not really fair that it is just you two."

She gives me a sad smile. "We tried for a while, but the pain of losing them time and time again was just too much. Alvin's cousin has an alpha son who will be moving in when he graduates high school. He wants to attend Michigan State University anyways, so it works for all of us."

"You aren't going to ask Max to take over?" I ask her in surprise. "I figured that was part of why you were so happy to find him alive. Don't all the supernaturals value bloodline and inheritance like that?"

Maria places her hand on mine and lets out a chuckle. "Oh, sweetie, we are just happy and excited that he is alive. That's the extent of our expectations," she says. "He has his position in his pack, his foundation and family, and *you*. You have your own responsibilities which means you can't be tied to a pack as an Alpha Mate.

Whereas, with my son as Head Warrior in the pack closest to your kingdom's headquarters, neither of you will have sacrifice duty for love unless you choose to."

I look at her in awe. She is willing to give up legacy so that we can have our love without encumbrances.

I wanna be Maria when I grow up…

My good mood quickly shifts to dread when the door opens. Max and Alpha Alvin enter, followed by four people who I have zero doubt as to their relation to my friend. Erica was merely a younger version of her mother. Her little sister has the same face, and her brother has those damn emerald eyes that match their father's.

It's time to let the Neeley family know why their daughter never came back home alive.

"Mr. Neeley," Max says as he sits next to me, "I will remind you once again, like I did outside, any insults against my mate will be equivalent to a declaration of war against me and my pack and the all of vampire kingdoms of this continent, so I will suggest you hold your tongue if you have nothing nice to say."

I turn to Max and send him the question, *What the fuck did he say to get that kind of a warning?*

My mate glances at me briefly but gives the family in front of him the full weight of his gaze.

He won't be repeating it, so it doesn't matter. Alpha Alvin has already threatened to kick the family out of the pack if he doesn't change his ways.

"I don't understand why we need a bloodsucker to tell us that Erica was killed by one," the teenage boy says in the silence. "The witch already told us that much. It's not like they'll ever give us the one who did it, so what the fuck is the point of this?"

"Jason Alexander Neeley!" his mother admonishes and smacks the boy upside his head. His wolf grumbles and flashes briefly in his eyes, but it's obvious he loves and respects his mother.

The name flashes me back to the lab for a second and I hear Erica's voice in my head.

"My parents fought over who got to name my brother. My mom wanted Alexander, but my dad wanted to name him Jason, after my grandfather.

They flipped a coin and Dad won. If I ever have a son, I'm naming him Alexander, in honor of my mother."

"Yeah, dummy," the younger girl sticks her tongue out at her brother pulling me back to the table. "You're gonna cause the Alpha to kick Daddy out and then I won't get any more pretty dresses."

Was that why Ethan named his boys Alec and Zander? Did he do it for Erica?

"No one cares about your dresses, pipsqueak," the boy says back. Their mother rolls her eyes and makes them separate, placing herself between them at the table.

"I apologize for my family, Alpha Snowden, Alpha Mate Maria, Prince Joshua, and Warrior Stephens," Mrs. Neeley says with more tact than the entire remaining members of her family combined have shown. "I only want answers as to what happened to my daughter. If they are disruptive to the process, I will send my family home."

"The fuck you will, Beverly! Erica was my daughter, too!" Mr. Neeley explodes to his feet. "I won't let the bloodsucker that killed her continue to exist, and if I have to deal with the prince of the fuckers to find the leech, then so be it. You will *not* cut me out!"

I can feel the panic rising in me. How am I supposed to tell this man that I killed her? I feel the grief pouring out of him. He doesn't hate vampires for no reason... As soon as I can take a good breath, I will tell them. They deserve to know...

"Mr. Neeley, you were warned," Max's voice comes from next to me, harsher than I have ever heard him. "Alpha, can I trouble your warriors for their assistance in detaining this man until King Edward can pass his judgment?"

51

MAX

I would find Josh's face humorous if it wasn't for the fact that I'm struggling to hold my wolf back from ripping open the dickwad in front of me. There is a difference between grief and stupidity and Mr. Neeley was warned three times. As the warriors drag him screaming from the room, Mrs. Neeley looks relieved while the two children stare at the door.

"Mrs. Neeley, are your children capable of behaving in here or would you prefer them to wait in the sitting room?" Alpha Alvin asks. "I do have some of the household betas on hand to keep an eye on them if you'd like."

She looks conflicted before speaking directly to my mate. "You already know what happened to Erica, don't you?"

Josh nods slowly, the fear is evident on his face, but the mother in front of us only nods her head. She instructs her children to go to the other room with the betas. Jason tries to argue, but he eventually gives in to his mother. When it is only her and us in the room, she puts her head in her hands and stares at the table.

"Tell me what happened to my little girl," she says in a choked whisper. The fact that she is hiding her tears is evident from the sudden strain on her voice. "I need to know. Is the one who killed her dead?"

Josh swallows a couple times, trying to speak, but nothing comes out. I know feels like he is the one that killed Erica, but I was in his head. I know what happened.

"Yes," I tell Mrs. Neeley and my mate smacks his hand against my chest in protest. "The two men who tortured your daughter to death and continued to torment her friends have died after a hell of a lot of pain. The man who employed them was killed personally by my Alpha just last month. All of the ones responsible have met their maker in extremely painful ways."

What are you doing? Josh sends to my mind. *Why are you lying to her?*

I turn to him and pull him into a soft kiss. *I'm not lying to her. She is asking about who is responsible, who killed Erica. You were a victim as much as she was.*

"But I drank her blood," he whimpers out loud and I hold his face so he can only look at me when the other people in the room react.

"You were bound with chains and she told you to do it. It was the only way for both of you to even try to get out of there alive and whole," I tell him, pulling him around so his back was to the grieving mother and my parents took the hint to stay out of his line of sight as well. "You took a sip, a fucking sip, and then those fuckers slit her throat with a silver dagger and hung her like a steer in a meat locker. They drained her blood over you while you couldn't get away."

I'm not able to hold back my own tears at this point and pull him into my chest in a crushing hug. "You fucking choked and drowned in her blood! They locked you in a coffin with her fucking corpse until your mind broke, baby, and I won't let you keep blaming yourself for what the fucking traitor and walking landfill did to all of you in there!"

I force myself to meet the eyes of Mrs. Neeley over his head and growl out through clenched teeth as I feel Josh's mind slip from the present, "No one else will ever touch a fucking hair on his head to harm him. Do you hear me?"

Mrs. Neeley wipes her eyes and nods at me. Her eyes drift down to the man in my arms who is now screaming into my chest while he relives the horror of that memory yet again. His claws are tearing up my back, but I shake my head in warning when my father moves toward us. This is why I didn't want to do this at all. It's tearing up my heart to hear the pain in my mate's voice, but I vow this is the very last time he will have to relive this for other people's benefit.

After a solid ten minutes of screaming, Josh manages to exhaust himself and passes out. Maria pulls some blankets and a pillow out of a cabinet, and I lay him gently on the floor in the corner where I can keep an eye on both him and the rest of the room. My wolf is worked up, and I need to make sure we all keep our cool. Once I'm sure my mate is safe, I remove the scraps that used to be one of my favorite t-shirts from Ethan.

"Do you need bandages?" Mrs. Neeley asks before looking at the sleeping vampire.

"I'll be fine," I bite out before I get a handle on my anger. The woman in front of me is not the one who deserves it. The ones who do are already dead and gone. Turning to my mother, I ask, "Do you have anything to clean up the blood and get the smell out of here before he wakes up? I don't want to set him off again when he realizes he cut me."

Maria and Alpha Alvin start grabbing things out of cabinets, and I grab some wet wipes from one of the cleaning kits. I crouch next to Josh and start gently wiping the blood from his fingertips, using my own nails to get the blood out from under his. Once I'm sure I got all of the blood off him, I make a second pass with the wipes just to make sure.

Throwing the bloody mess in a bag to be taken from the room, I catch a glimpse of Mrs. Neeley's face. She looks conflicted, and I raise my eyebrow at her. Yeah, it sucks that her daughter died. She seemed like an awesome girl based on what I've seen of her through Josh and Ethan's memories, but they are fucking lucky she died in there.

"Say whatever you want to fucking say, lady," I tell her as I pull on a fresh shirt that the Alpha hands me. The scratches weren't deep and stopped bleeding quickly. "You don't know how fortunate you are to not have to watch the people you love morph into these terrified animals, acting purely on survival instinct, fighting against evil that you can't even kill because it's already dead."

There is a collective gasp from the women in the room, but the Alpha just glances at the huddled form of my mate under the blankets.

"I personally ended the two fuckers who murdered your daughter, but my mate still lives that moment over and over every time he smells blood," I stalk toward her and she raises her face to meet mine. "Can you even imagine the pain he is in every fucking day? He's a fucking vampire! Blood is life for them, but he can't be around it because those assholes used your daughter's death to make him fear what he needs to live!"

Her arms wrapping around me takes me by surprise. My knees give out and somehow this woman has enough strength to gently lower us to our knees on the floor. My heart rips open inside of my chest, and I sob like I haven't done since that night in the tub, watching the pink water turn clear.

52

JOSH

I open my eyes as soon as I realize I am awake, worried that I left my mate alone to face the consequences of my actions. But he's right next to me in bed. We're laying diagonally across the queen size bed in the suite his mother put us in last night. Was that all just a really vivid nightmare? It started off so great with French toast and jokes about the Alpha getting old when he complained about wishing he could still get an actual newspaper delivered instead of having to use the tablet.

"You're up?" Max mumbles on a yawn and starts running his hand up and down my arm. "I think it's still early enough we can get some dinner if you're up for it."

I hum in appreciation before I sit up in a rush. "Dinner?!"

Grabbing my phone from the side table, I look at the time:

5:48 PM

"So that wasn't a dream? Mrs. Neeley knows what happened to Erica?"

Max nods as he sits up to pull me into his lap. "She knows the truth of what happened, not just what your guilt lets you tell yourself.

And she forgives you for your part in it, even though we all agree that there is nothing to forgive."

I'm in shock. There's no way Erica's family doesn't blame me. "What about Mr. Neeley?"

Max snorts and sets me down so he can walk over to our bags. When he's crouching in front of his to pick a shirt, I notice the raised red lines on his back. Did I do that? I stare at my fingertips, trying to find a trace of the blood I know I must have drawn, but there is nothing.

"The asshole wanted his Alpha to hold you in prison for him until he could *"verify our story"* about the lab," Max says bringing my attention back to him. He covered himself with a clean shirt, and I might be slightly incoherent still because I'm not exactly following.

"Of course, when my father suggested that Mr. Neeley petition your uncle with that request, the man looked like he was going to shit himself. Then I revealed Alpha Alvin as my father and asked if it would be grounds for an Alpha challenge if he were to imprison my mate, and the Mr. Neeley actually fainted."

Max threw a shirt at me with a laugh before sitting next to me on the bed. "Alice, that's Mrs. Neeley's first name by the way, has decided to contract a witch to break their bond since it was only a chosen mate bond. She is bringing the kids with her to South Carolina. She wants to be closer to the last people to know her daughter. Ric is giving her provisional status in the pack and will re-evaluate her status when it comes time for Amber to get her wolf."

"What about Jason? Isn't his wolf a member of this pack?" I ask while pulling on the shirt that is way too big for me. I remember him explaining about first shifts and belonging, so I have to assume that changing packs is a bit of a big deal.

Max pulls me into his side, burying his nose in my shoulder to sniff. "I love seeing you in my clothes," he says before straightening up.

"As for Jason, he was given the choice of staying with his father, who may or may not have a pack to belong to if he doesn't wise up quickly, or going with his mother to petition to belong to the Jameson pack. He chose his mother and sister."

As we head down the stairs toward the kitchen, I feel the need to voice some concerns. "Do you think your father would have really kicked a fourteen-year-old boy out of the pack just because *his* father is a disrespectful dumbass?"

"Absolutely," the Alpha's voice says from the sitting room as we are about to walk past. "I don't take in underage wolves without a guardian, and if no one volunteered to be one for him, he would have been shipped off to the closest pack where he had family. That would just happen to be his mother in the Jameson pack."

He winks at me before setting his tablet on the mantle. "By the way, dinner is at six, so you guys are just in time."

53

MAX

Family dinner is bittersweet for me. I love that I'm finally getting to experience this, but I know I'm going to have to disappoint both them and myself. I can't stay here beyond a visit. I can't be their next Alpha. I won't abandon the family I already have for the one that lost me so long ago.

"And of course, we want to meet Anna's children," Maria's voice cuts into my thoughts. Wait? How much have I missed in this conversation?

"Grandchildren, now," Josh tells her as he scoops more mashed potatoes onto his plate. "Ethan, my cousin, is mated to Ric, that's Alaric, Anna's older son, and he gave birth to triplets in August."

"Triplets, huh?" Alpha Alvin mutters before shoveling a piece of broccoli in his mouth. After he finishes chewing, he adds, "I guess it skips a generation then. You guys aren't planning on having kids, right?"

I start choking on the piece of chicken I tried to inhale in response to my father's question, and Josh slaps me on the back until I clear my airway.

"There's no such thing as a vampire omega," he tells the table. "So, if we want kids, we have to use a surrogate and it wouldn't likely take without major magical mojo to back it up. Wolves can't make babies without their marked mate, and vampire women can only give birth to their mate's kids. Hybrids can only happen naturally when it comes to vampires cuz unless it's a mate, no one else can carry the undead."

He shovels another mouthful of potatoes before continuing. "But since we're not taking over here, I can just wait until my Mama gets baby fever again to handle the whole heir thing. We don't need to have kids for any legacy reasons."

I do a double take at his words. "We aren't taking over here?" I turn to the Alpha. "You don't want me to be the Alpha Heir?"

Alpha Alvin laughs in response. "I've already promised the son of my cousin that he will be my heir. He's an alpha wolf with the Snowden name and close enough in appearance that no one will question him taking over after me. His wolf isn't as big or strong as yours, but he's on par with me. You were meant to be more than just an Alpha. You were meant to be the mate of a prince."

I jump up and run around the table to hug the man who gave me life. I see Maria wiping tears from her cheeks and I rush to hug her as well before sitting back down. Knowing that they understand and aren't going to try to force me into staying, I can finally eat my meal with gusto.

"This chicken is really good, Mama," I say before silence descends on the table. I look up and only realize what I just said when I see the shocked smiles on their faces.

"Thank you, sweetheart," she says with tears falling. "Eat up. We have the New Moon celebration tonight and then you two have a long drive home tomorrow."

I'm sure my eyes are a bit glassy as well as I dig in to my dinner.

54

MAX

Driving past the "Welcome to South Carolina" sign, I glance over at Josh in the passenger seat. He fell back asleep shortly after we left Ohio, and I decided to power through driving and let him sleep. The twelve hours behind the wheel have been exhausting, but worth it knowing that I'm taking care of my mate.

The center console lights up showing a call coming through from Ric and I rush to pick it up before it wakes him.

"Heads up that Josh is asleep, so I want to keep this short and quiet," I tell him on a whisper. "We're about an hour away if you think it can wait."

I hear the background noise muffle and a door close over the speakers before Ric says anything. "We're in the office and you're on speaker with me and Ethan. The babies are quiet for now, but no guarantees on how long it will last.

"What's your assessment of my mother's family?" he asks after a pause. "Jack found out where you went somehow and started to snoop around. Someone let it slip to him that my mother was originally from Michigan and now I've got a nine-year-old emotionally blackmailing me. *I* only know where my mother was from since I went looking for it. I have no clue who told Jack."

While I'm debating how much to tell my Alpha over the phone, Josh pipes up from beside me.

"Your aunt and uncle are alright people, but your cousin can be a really huge dick."

I start coughing in an attempt to hide my laughter and almost run the car off the road before getting under control. I glance over to see my mate looking at me with a mischievous smirk, so I stick my tongue out at him. I'm glad to see this lighthearted side of Josh.

"How big of a dick can he be?" Ethan asks, not catching the reference. "I mean, we have a few of those in the pack, so it's not like we can't put him in his place. Let *me* at him. I'll straighten him out."

Josh covers his mouth with his hands in a futile attempt to keep his laughter inside. My eyes are watering with my own struggles. Hell, I never would have considered this as a prank to play on my Alpha. But it's fucking hilarious!

"He is pretty big," I say as I take the exit ramp for the highway that runs closest to the pack. "But I don't think you could do anything to straighten him out, Little Dude. I am pretty sure that won't work with him."

Cuz you're not straight? Josh sends to my mind and proceeds to snort audibly.

That's apparently the last straw for both of us and we explode in laughter for a few minutes. When I can finally feel like I can breathe again, I look down at the console screen and see the call is still connected. Ethan and Ric were being really quiet while we were laughing like hyenas.

"You done?" the Alpha asks with irritation clear in his voice.

"Sorry, Boss-Man," I tell him while Josh hands me an open bottle of water. "My mate apparently thought it was funny to tease you about your cousin. It's good to see him happy."

"I didn't even know I had a cousin," Ric says. "Mom never talked about her family. Only reason I even knew there was more than Uncle Aaron was because I overheard him arguing with my dad that they should be allowed to go to their brother's Alpha ceremony. That was when we were like ten or so."

"So, when do we meet this giant dick of a cousin?" Ethan pipes up, breaking the serious mood. "And why can't I straighten him out?"

Josh and I meet each other's eyes and start laughing again. Over the call, Ethan makes a harumpf sound and the soft thud over the speakers tells me he's plopped down somewhere in the office to pout because we are laughing at him.

"Easy, Little Dude," I say as I pull up to a red light. "No need to throw a fit. You'll never straighten him out."

"Yeah, Cuz," Josh chimes in. "I don't think his mate would like it if he suddenly became straight. It would put a rather *huge* damper on their bedroom time."

I choke on my water, thankful the light is still red so that I can recover without needing to buy my Alpha a new car. Ethan is on the other side of the phone giggling, and I can almost picture Ric shaking his head in annoyance.

"Another one for team dick!" Ethan yells out and starts humming the theme song for some wrestler's entrance. Bastian has introduced him to professional wrestling and this song is for favorite. I am afraid it has now become the theme song for "team dick" as he has coined it.

While Ethan is humming and I'm assuming dancing in the background, Ric asks, "So now that you've had your fun, do we have to go to them or will they come to us to meet?"

"Well that's the thing, Boss-Man. You've already met your cousin," I tell him and can't resist having a bit more fun at his expense. "We're about to hit a dead zone. I... at... later... now you know."

I hit the disconnect icon on the screen and laugh along with Josh as Ric's name keeps flashing up on the screen. We are roughly a half an hour from the pack border, and another fifteen to twenty to the Alpha's house. It's kind of fun messing around with him like this, knowing he's family and I belong in ways I never did before.

55

JOSH

Waking up and messing with my cousin's mate, who happens to also be my mate's cousin, was a blast and kept me from really worrying about what happened this last week in Michigan. Maria and Alvin are wonderful people, and it was a horrible tragedy that they didn't get to raise the man sitting next to me. But if they had raised him, would I have met him? Would I have met Ethan?

"We will be at the house in about fifteen," Max announces as he turns on yet another random street within the Jameson pack territory. We just passed the football stadium. "What's got that look on your face?"

I glance over at him and notice him looking at me, so I give him a smile.

"I was just thinking that if you weren't raised where you were by that woman, we probably never would have met." He gives me a questioning glance in response and makes a left turn at the next intersection. Holy fuck, the roads in this pack are a maze.

"What makes you say that?"

I take a minute to gather my thoughts before answering him.

"Alright, I'll try to explain," I tell him and turn sideways in my seat to face him. We're going at most thirty-five miles per hour so even if he wrecks, it would barely cause a scratch. "If Alvin and Maria hadn't lost you, they would have raised you in Michigan and you'd have been raised as the Alpha Heir, having zero contact with the Jameson pack because of Ric's father's asshole-ish ways, right? You wouldn't know Ric or Connor. You'd never save Ethan.

"Maybe you'd meet my uncle during his little tour every twenty years or so, but generally if there's no issues, he just passes through an area without stopping. And his last trip was right around the time Ethan was sold to the lab. So, we wouldn't have met that way."

He purses his lips as he makes another seemingly random turn, but I can tell he is following along.

"And let's say Ethan survived everything without your help and ended up in the lab. I would meet him in there, but he wouldn't have the skills you taught him. Then, let's assume we get out of the lab the same way: Me getting gutted and found by my family while Ethan gets rescued by Connor. Ethan and I maybe reconnect since we are in the same area, but no one is there to keep me from going off the deep end. My guilt gets the better of me, and I submit myself to the Neeley family. Mr. Neeley would want my death and it would have happened because you wouldn't speak up for a stranger. You wouldn't be a part of the meeting. The only reason the Alpha was there this time was because of you being there. We would have never happened..."

I look out the windshield when Max stops the car. We have apparently arrived at the house. Ethan bounces down the front steps to come over to the car, while Ric alternates between showing affection and annoyance on his face. Hell, that seems to be his natural default when he isn't being possessed by his dead pseudo mother-in-law.

"You forget something, Little One," Max says as he pulls me over to touch his forehead to mine. "We are fated mates. There is a reason Erica was from the Snowden pack. No matter what, I have always been meant to save you from yourself. There will never be a reality where I will allow you to be punished for evil men's actions."

Before I can fully process what he means, he slams his lips to mine and takes my mouth in a possessive claiming. To call it a kiss would be like calling Lake Erie a puddle...

Understatement of the century.

56

JOSH

My memory is a bit hazy on how I got from the car to Ric's office. The kiss that Max planted on me kind of made my brain do a hard reboot. I *think* I walked myself into the house, but I can honestly say I am not one hundred percent sure of that.

So, are you guys like mates like friends or mates like bumping uglies now?

I almost miss the seat of the sofa when Ethan's voice pops into my head and I turn around too quickly to make eye contact with him. He giggles and grabs a couple juice boxes out of the mini fridge Ric put in the corner. My cousin took exception to the fact that his Alpha only had the wet bar in his office and decided that there needed to be child friendly options. Actually, he thought there needed to be options for his own little side so he could hang out with his Daddy in the office.

Can you ever speak properly? I send to him as I feel underneath my butt before sitting to make sure I'm not going to plant my ass on the floor. *And give me soda. I'll down that juice box in two seconds.*

"Here you are, good sir," Ethan says to me in his terrible example of a British accent. He almost sounds Australian, and I have to laugh.

"Thanks, Crocodile Dundee," I say as I take the soda can from his outstretched hand. He rises up from his bow with a questioning look. Max and Ric both laugh with me at my cousin's obvious confusion.

Ethan plops on the floor in a huff and mumbles, "Not my fault I missed movies for most of the first twenty-one years of my life."

Max sits next to me on the sofa and throws his arm over my shoulder while Ric sits on the loveseat across from us. When he pats his leg, Ethan crawls up into his mate's lap like a little toddler.

"We aren't laughing at your ignorance, Blue," Ric explains, combing his fingers through Ethan's red curls. "Josh was just referencing a movie from way before any of us was born. It's about a guy who is from the Australian outback who comes to New York and ends up solving crimes or something. It's a truly terrible example of how little taste people had back in the eighties."

Ethan pops his thumb out of his mouth to ask, "Can we watch it later, Daddy?"

We all chuckle and Ric tells him he'll look up what streaming service might have it once we finish our talk. Ethan pops his thumb back into his mouth and leans down on Ric's chest again, effectively leaving the rest of the words for the adults, or rather those of us still thinking like adults.

"So now that there is no way to pretend you've lost cell service, how about you tell me about my family that has stayed away my entire life?" Ric glares at us while keeping his voice light. We all try to keep things from getting heavy when Ethan is in his little space.

I tense up, but my mate relaxes further into the furniture. *Is it a good idea to be disrespectful to your Alpha even though you're family now? He doesn't know that yet and I like all of your limbs attached.*

Max chuckles next to me and nuzzles the mark he left on my neck before sending me a message of his own. *I'm disrespectful at best on most days. If I'm too serious, Ric will worry and that will freak Ethan out. So, I am being the typical smartass me.*

"So here's the thing, Boss-Man," Max tells Ric, pulling his arm from around me to lean forward in his seat. "Your mother was actually the middle child in a set of triplets... two boys and a girl. Sound familiar?"

Ethan's eyes get really big and he sits up looking back and forth between his mate and mine. He looks like he almost wants to say something, but instead he starts actively sucking his thumb.

"Your grandparents, who have passed by the way, only had the triplets. Alvin Snowden is the current Alpha of the Snowden pack in Michigan. His mate is named Maria. Their son has rejected the position of Alpha Heir due to his mate and responsibilities elsewhere. Alvin has named the alpha son of a cousin as his heir and the boy will be moving in when he graduates high school next year."

Ric looks a bit conflicted with this news. I can't tell if he's upset about never knowing his grandparents or the fact that his uncle had to choose an heir because his cousin isn't taking over there.

"Your mother, Ms. Annabelle Snowden-Jameson, had left home at eighteen to seek out her mate as is the custom in their pack," Max continues. "Apparently, it's like the Amish humans' thing where they leave for a year to find their future outside and return if they don't find their mate. Sometimes they will return with their mate, but most of the women stay with their mate's pack. When Anna didn't come home and they didn't hear from her after a year had passed, Aaron left to look for their sister."

Ric seems to be struggling with hearing about his mother. I never knew the woman, and my only knowledge of her is what Max has shared with me. She was his angel. She created Jack, who is probably the purest soul I have met outside of newborns. Even if that was all she ever accomplished, I will forever regard that woman as one of the highest caliber.

"The only word Alvin received was a single letter from Aaron," my mate's voice breaks through my thoughts. "The letter was informing him that Anna found her mate and that he was staying with her as protection. He promised he would bring her home as soon as he could convince her to leave. That letter was dated almost twenty-seven years ago. They knew she was mated, and that Aaron did not like him."

I grab Max's hand in solidarity while he is speaking, but I can't look away from Ric. I don't know what his memories are of his mother, but he there is obvious pain wrapped up with what he is hearing. Ethan has curled back against his mate's chest; a faraway and sad look has taken over his face.

"Why didn't they ever come for her... for us?" the Alpha asks in a soft voice, and I feel my heart breaking a little bit for him. I didn't mean to hear it, but inside his head, he is screaming: *Why didn't they want us? Why didn't they save us?*

Ethan meets my eyes, and I know he hears it as well.

57

MAX

My mate squeezing my hand makes me look up from the table where I've been staring. I have been purposely avoiding looking at anyone so that I could get the facts out without revealing too much of my own feelings on things. Josh lifts his chin toward the loveseat. When I see my Alpha and his mate, I realize that in protecting myself, I am hurting them. It's time to let them know everything and who I am. If I lose what I have, maybe at least they'll get the closure they need.

Taking a deep breath, I sit up straight and grasp my mate's hand in both of mine. It's now or never.

"They didn't know about you," I tell him and watch the shadows move in his eyes. There is anger and pain, but I can recognize the sliver of relief. I went through it myself a few days ago.

"Alvin and Maria were pregnant around the same time your mother was. It was a difference of only a few months, and the only one who knew was Aaron. Alvin and Maria told him they were expecting, but Aaron wrote back to tell them he would let them know when they could bring the baby to visit since your father was not allowing outsiders to enter the pack.

"From what I understand, your mother was having a difficult pregnancy, so my speculation is that Aaron didn't want to stress his sister out by telling her about their family back in Michigan when there was nothing to be done. Neither woman could travel, and Alvin couldn't leave his pregnant mate behind to see his sister. So, it's safe to assume Aaron took it upon himself and kept the truth from both of his siblings for the sake of their unborn children.

"Then, Alvin and Maria lost their child. They were told by the doctors their baby had been still-born, dead before he could take his first breath."

Ethan's gasp pulls my gaze away from Ric to see him bury himself deeper into his Daddy's arms. I sometimes forget that he lost the first baby he conceived with Ric since the triplets are here and healthy. Ethan never really had the opportunity to mourn or grieve for that baby properly.

He's looking for a therapist to talk about all of it, Josh's voice comes into my head. *He promised Ric he will try as long as he doesn't have to go to the hospital for it.*

"But you said you know Daddy's cousin?" Ethan's question is barely comprehensible with how muffled his voice is, but I answer him anyways. It's time to stop drawing it out.

"I know him very well, Little Dude," I tell him and wait for him to turn and meet my eyes. "Because he is me."

58

MAX

To say that they didn't believe it would be an understatement. Ethan alternates between being excited and dubious. Meanwhile Ric is clearly skeptical of my statement.

Why does the Alpha look like he's constipated? Josh sends to me as he reaches for his drink.

I huff a soft laugh before lifting his hand to plant a kiss on the back of it. *That's his thinking face, Little One.*

My mate turns to look at me in surprise and give him a peck on the cheek for being so adorable right now. Never in a million years did I think I would find a boy of my own, let alone one as perfect as the man in front of me.

"I can show you if you think we're lying," Josh tells them when no one speaks for a while. "Your friend Cassie popped in to show all of us what happened back then. Shark Bitch and Doctor Douche fucked up Max's life long before fucking around with us."

Ethan rolls off his Daddy's lap in a fit of giggles while Ric just raises an eyebrow. He looks back and forth between us as if trying to spot a falsehood.

"Shark Bitch!" Ethan gasps out from the floor as he tries to regain some sort of composure. "I really shouldn't laugh. That was a really terrible thing I did, but fuck if that name isn't gonna stick."

Ric nods at my mate, and Josh shares his memory of witnessing the events from my birth. I don't need to see it again, so I watch my best friends' reactions. Ric runs through his usual anger and super-hero complex. He is a justice warrior, only he doesn't always see clearly what justice is. Ethan on the other hand, looks so sad.

I hate that discovering my identity is making him relive something no one should ever have to experience. If this world was fair, parents wouldn't lose their kids. The pain on my Little Dude's face is too much for me to see. I give Josh's hand a squeeze before I stand to move to the window, letting the world fall away for a while.

A few minutes later, I feel a small hand on my lower back. When I turn around, it's only Ethan and I in the room. I don't know when our mates left. I must have been really deep in my own head to have missed it.

You need to talk things out with him, Josh's voice flows into my head. *He is your little brother after all, right?*

Pulling Ethan into a hug, I send my love to my mate. He's right. This is a conversation that is long overdue.

"Are you big now?" I ask the man in my arms with a peck to the top of his head. "We need to have grown up talk now."

Ethan steps away from me and looks up. I still hate the fact that he is so small and won't get any bigger. Being stuck in that lab during his teenage years means that instead of his body having the growth spurts it should have, it was focused on healing damage. His father and grandfather are both over six foot, but Ethan tops out at five foot four, on a good day.

"You know I would bring them back to kill them slower if I could," I growl under my breath, and my wolf hums in agreement.

Ethan giggles and heads back to the loveseat. "I could probably do that, actually," he says as he flops down, spreading out across the entire length of the cushions, his feet dangling over the side. "But they need to stay in the bad place where you sent them."

I sit back on the sofa across from him and struggle with where I want to start. For so much of my life, my focus was either survival or protecting someone else, mainly the man in front of me. He was my drive, my passion. Hell, he was my will to live for a while.

"You have to live for yourself now, Max," he says in an uncharacteristically serious tone. "I love you. I really do. You're my big brother in ways that Connor never was and never could be."

He sits up quickly and waves his hands like he needs to take back what he just said. "Not that Connie isn't a great big brother. But he is the Wally to my Beaver. But you? You were in the trenches with me. You taught me things that I needed to know. You gave me the tools to survive."

He wrings his hands together, staring at table between us. It takes him a moment to gather his thoughts before he speaks again.

"Connie faced his own struggles. I always knew that. He tried his best, but Fake Mom made it her personal goal to keep him too busy to see me, spend time with me. I knew how much it bothered him to not have time for me, so I hid a lot from him. You were there to pick up the slack. You didn't just save me that day in the alley. You showed me that there are people who might actually care what happened to me. You became closer to me than my own family."

We stare at each other for a while. I don't know how much time has actually passed when my mate breaks in using the mind speak.

If you guys are done with your heart to heart, I would like to get back to the apartment where we can have some crazy loud sex and make Chase extremely uncomfortable.

I laugh out loud and notice Ethan's eyes are huge.

Uh, Baby? I think your cousin heard that.

I feel his embarrassment before he disconnects and I stand up, holding my hand out to Ethan. He takes it and we walk to the office door, hand in hand. I chuckle at the fact that I'm blessed with a mate who understands our connection.

"Uh, Max?" Ethan pulls me to a stop before I get the door open. "I want to ask you something important before we go out there."

Turning to him, I kneel down in front of him so he doesn't have to look up to ask me. If someone were looking in, it would look like I'm proposing to him, but the people who matter know that this is just because he is too damn short.

"I was going to ask Shaun, but with how everything is with him and Connie, I don't want to make things awkward and risk one of them not showing up," he starts rambling and I'm already lost.

"Well, I guess I could, but then Ric would ask you most likely, but I want you up there next to me. But I want Shaun there too and Connie and Jackie..."

I put my hand over his mouth and wait for him to take a breath. "What do you want, Little Dude?"

"Will you be my best man?"

I fall back onto my ass in front of him. Never in a million years did I think I would be close enough to someone to be asked this. But he's right. His best friend is Shaun, and I know he would regret it if the doc wasn't up there with him. Same way I know Ric would regret if Connor wasn't standing next to him.

"How about this?" I say when my silence causes sadness to creep into Ethan's baby blues. "I'll get ordained online and perform the ceremony so that we can all be up there together. That way, you won't have to choose between me and your bestie and your brother."

That's how, less than a minute later, Ric opens the door to find us laying on the floor, laughing after I got tackled by one hundred forty pounds of omega twink.

59

JOSH

After Ethan and Max finish their talk, we decide to leave our bags in the car and take his motorcycle back to my apartment. We will be back in the morning, or at least Max will, to take Jack to school. So, it's not that big of a deal to leave the bags where they are for now.

About an hour after sunset, we pull into the complex. Looking around, I'm surprised to see a moving truck by the front door, but I don't really worry about it. People move at all hours of the day. It's not until we are heading into the building and see Chase coming down the stairs carrying a box that I even consider what this could mean.

"What the fuck do you think you're doing?" I demand as I stomp away from my mate to confront him.

The bastard only laughs at me as he walks to the back of the truck to set the box inside. After brushing his hands off on his pants, he comes over to us, offering his hand to Max to shake. My mate takes it reluctantly, confusion clear on his face.

"I've got orders from the king to give you two your space for a while," he says throwing me a wink. "Two kings, actually, and a very upset Mama who wants to know why her baby boy didn't tell her he found his mate."

Oh, fuck!

I completely forgot to tell my parents about Max. I didn't want to tell them when I thought he rejected me because then my older brothers would have come out to hunt his ass down, not to mention Mama...

And we only recently cleared everything up and then the battle and the trip and finding out my mate's past...

"How much does Mama know?" I ask with a wince.

Chase gives me a sympathetic look and turns back to close the back of the truck. "Enough to have bought a house and land just outside of Jameson Pack territory big enough for you two to have your privacy with an in-law suite for her to drop in whenever the fuck she wants."

When she wants? I can't stop the thought from escaping.

Chase tosses the keys to Max, and he catches them by reflex.

"She'll be here in the morning," my friend says as he heads back to the stairs, patting my shoulder on his way past. "Address and house keys are on the dash. I'm keeping the Blu-ray collection and the bean bag chairs. Everything else is packed or already there."

I'm not sure how long I'm staring at the empty stairs, but Max reaches over to push my jaw up to close my mouth. Looking over at him, he chuckles at my deer in the headlights look.

"I guess now it's my turn to meet the in-laws," he says, pressing a kiss to my forehead. "Let's go break in our new house before they descend on us."

Max leads me to the cab of the moving truck and lifts me into the passenger side. When he gets in the driver's seat, I come out of my stupor. My parents bought us a house. Not only that, but they bought it knowing exactly where Max can still be a part of his pack without me having to sacrifice my own position. I sniffle and promise to give Mama a super duper mega hug when I see her tomorrow.

60

MAX

I was putting on a brave face yesterday when I found out that I would be meeting my mate's family. In reality, I'm fucking terrified. Having spent time with King Edward, I am worried about being in the same house as King Seamus and his mate Isobel and any other members of the family that might be deciding to join them. Josh seems more agitated than usual, so I am doing my best to hold myself together for his sake.

"Do you think we should have offered to pick them up from the airport?" Josh asks me as he straightens up the kitchen counter for the tenth time this morning. "We should have, right?"

I pull him into my arms to stop his fidgeting. "We don't have a car yet, remember? I only have my motorcycle and you never bothered to get a vehicle of your own since Chase was always driving you around."

I walk him out into the living room and push him down to sit on the sofa. "I plan on us taking your mother out to help us pick one out. I've heard that letting my mother-in-law have a say in inconsequential things will make it easier for her to accept it when she isn't part of other decisions."

My mate starts laughing so hard that he collapses to his side on the couch. The laughter goes on long enough that he is gasping for air, tears streaming down his cheeks.

"Oh, you innocent boy!" he finally manages to gasp out. "Mama is a Latina madre! You give her an inch, she will never leave. I'm already going to have to figure out how to point out that buying this house was overstepping without insulting her. There is no fucking way she is going to have a hand in picking out anything else for us. We are NOT taking her car shopping."

I smile at his adamance concerning getting his mother's opinion. Granted, I'm not all that familiar with his mother's culture, but I don't think it could be all that bad. At least I managed to snap him out of his constant worry and fidgeting before they arrive. And it's not a moment too soon since I hear tires on the gravel outside.

Josh stops laughing when he hears it and rushes to the front porch. The wrap-around is probably my favorite feature of this house. I'll never tell Ric this, but his house is a travesty and modern monstrosity. *This* house is the classic southern design I've always wanted, sitting on a small rise with actual functioning storm shutters and a wrap-around porch facing east to watch the sunrise over the treetops.

I come outside and wrap my arms around my mate from behind. I can feel the nerves and indecision radiating off of him, so I take the choices away from him. If his family has an issue with him not helping unload, they can blame me.

I don't have to worry about blame when a woman about the same size as Ethan practically flies out of the backseat to crush both of us in a hug.

"Hijo, you should have told me you found your mate!" she shakes her finger up into Josh's face as soon as she releases us. "Why did I have to find out from your stuffy old fuddy duddy uncle?"

"Please stop calling my big brother a fuddy duddy, Mi Amor," a man's voice, heavy with an Irish accent, calls from the trunk area of the car. "Eddie can't help that the stick is permanently stuck up his arse."

I choke on a laugh and realize that what I've always imagined for a possible future was so far off the mark. Family, love, friends... How in the fuck did I end up with something so wonderful?

61

JOSH

I was worried for nothing. My parents coming is exactly what I needed. And I think they broke my mate. Max has been quietly smiling since they got here this morning. He, thankfully, didn't take my mother car shopping, but Dad went with him to pick out a couple options. They found out about each other's appreciation of custom motorcycles, so my mate is going to take Dad to his guy to see about getting something built for when they come out to visit next time.

That left me at home with Mama. I've missed my mother so much, but I didn't know how to handle keeping secrets from her. That's the only reason why I stayed away for so long.

"I'm sorry, Mama," I blurt out as she is taking her oatmeal chocolate chip cookies from the oven. She has insisted that Max is too thin and needs fattening up. I disagree, but I think it's engrained in her that when in doubt, feed them.

"What are you apologizing for, mi niño?"

I wait for her to put the cookies on the cooling rack. "I have been hiding from you, Mama. I'm so sorry."

I rush over and wrap my arms around her, curling over her, wishing I was still the little boy that fit so perfectly in her arms. "It hurt so much. I didn't want you to hurt with me, so I ran and hid from everyone."

Her hands run up and down my back as I release all of my guilt and pain. This is why I haven't been home since I recovered physically. My mother would have never let me leave her side if she knew what I was hiding. I'm practically falling apart in her arms, and this is with improvement.

"Oh, honey," she croons as she pushes away enough to wipe my tears away. "I was only waiting for you to come to me. You try so hard to be macho, hombre like your hermanos. But you feel much deeper than them. You suffered more than them. You survived more than they ever will."

I see nothing but love and pride on her face when she adds in a conspiratorial whisper, "Plus, your brothers' mates are boring white women who are lovely to look at, but have no flair. Your mate is so much better. He has a sense of humor, is extremely protective of you, and let's face it – looking at him is definitely not a chore."

"Mama!" I cry out in shock as I step back. "You are mated! Keep your eyes off my man!"

She shrugs and moves to put the next tray of cookies in the oven. "I'm mated, not dead. You found yourself a looker, and as your mother, it is my right to take a good *long* look."

I collapse onto a stool at the coffee bar when her meaning sinks in. With exasperation, I remind my mother, "You, know it is highly inappropriate to be thinking about the penis of your youngest son's mate."

She just laughs and pushes me to the side to brew herself a cup of coffee. I smile at her, knowing that everything is still good between us, and for the first time in years, I feel close to being whole.

EPILOGUE
MAX

Hurry up, Papi!

Josh's voice rings in my head. He started calling me that right around Christmas time after he overheard his sister call her mate that as a joke. I like it a lot. It satisfies my inner Daddy while still respecting that our relationship isn't the strict dynamic like what our cousins live.

"Hold your horses!" I yell from the workshop as I grab the last of the presents for the triplets. They are turning one today, and we promised we would be at the house early to help with set up. The therapist Josh started to see suggested he pick up a hobby to help with the anxiety and panic attacks. After trying things like needle-work and crochet, which were abysmal failures that killed multiple robot vacuums, he found that woodworking and woodburning were his niche.

The handmade rocking horses that he crafted for the babies are gorgeous and already in the back of the truck. I just picked up the hand carved decorative blocks he finally finished last night. Each letter is burned into the block, along with a depiction of a word beginning with that letter. The wood for these presents came from the trees we cleared to make room for our newly built guest house.

I didn't realize that by buying us the house, my in-laws took it upon themselves to use our house as a hotel whenever they would decide to come out to the east coast. After the third time waking up to my mother-in-law cooking us breakfast, I decided we needed an external structure for them to stay in. The new building has electronic locks, so we don't have to worry about giving out keys. Each couple or person has their own code, and we can keep track of who is visiting when.

"Papi! We're gonna be late!" Josh calls out as I come around the corner of the house. He is already at the passenger door of the SUV. "I already heard the Ducati go past and I don't want to have Connor and Shaun beat us there! I want first snuggles with the birthday brats."

I put the box of blocks in the backseat and climb in the front. Even though they have Shaun's coworker and good friend acting as a surrogate, heavily pregnant at that, the two of them still bicker and fight in public. Most of us recognize that it is all a type of foreplay for them, but Ric and Ethan don't seem to catch on. In all fairness, they *have* been distracted with the babies.

"I'm sure we will be the first to arrive," I tell him, climbing into the driver's seat.

The drive over to the house is quiet in the early morning, so when I see Seb's truck around the back of the Alpha's house, curiosity takes precedence over courtesy. Josh takes my hand as we walk around the outside and my jaw drops at the sight in front of me.

Seb has used the winch on his truck to drag Connor's motorcycle from the swimming pool.

I turn to see the Alpha with his boys, Alec and Zander, on each of his hips while Ethan has little Tessa in his arms. The babies look sleepy, but Ric and Ethan look concerned.

"Is everyone alright?" I ask and they startle as if they didn't notice us walk up.

"We don't know," Ethan whispers. "Someone drove the bike here and crashed it, but no one was out here when Ric saw it in the pool."

"I could have sworn I heard it pass by our house not even fifteen minutes before we left," Josh says as he takes Alec from his father. "I figured it was Connor or Shaun on their way here."

"We don't know who it was," Ric says and meets my gaze. "And that fact worries me."

ABOUT THE AUTHOR

I am a dog mom living it up in the insanity that is Northeast Ohio. When I'm not documenting the exploits of the characters in my head, I'm either binge reading the works of other amazing authors or losing my voice at hockey games. I'm horribly addicted to coffee, anime, and Asian dramas in addition to building my ever-growing stuffie army.

K.A. Bauer is the paranormal alter ego of Kate Bauer. I guess you could say Kate lives in this reality while K.A. is in a reality where mythical creatures and magic exist, and fate makes finding true love easier. All of her stories are LGBTQIA+ centric, and the characters fight for their rights and happily ever afters.

For the latest news on releases and appearances, check out my website www.authorkabauer.com

I can be found on most social media sites under the username @authorkabauer

KATE BAUER BOOKS

Manor Drive Series
A Little Discovery
Drag Me Up
Pet Project
Teddy Tea Time
Night Shift
No Pain, No Gain

Up/Down Series
Stood Up
Let Down
Trade Up

Wrenshaw University Series
Freshman Fifteen
Injured Reserve
Professor's Pet
Too Many Men

MR DRAG Series
Wish Upon DeStarr

K.A. BAUER BOOKS

Alpha's Little Psycho Series
Alive
Holly Jolly Psycho (Novella)
Unburied
Afraid
Complete Series Omnibus

Jameson Pack Series
Fated Mistake
Doctor Mate
Half Mate
Learned Fate

www.ingramcontent.com/pod-product-compliance
Lightning Source LLC
Chambersburg PA
CBHW051341020726
47501CB00007B/2202